WARNING

If you are a parent or a teacher, [or anyone] over eighteen, put this book down [now. You] won't like it. You won't understand it. You will be totally grossed out by it.

The book is chock-full of buttosaurs, farthropods, stinksects, buttphibians, stenchtiles, invertebutts, butt-fish, and bummals. It has detailed illustrations of Poopigator, Fartosaurus, Toiletrollasaurus, Buttadactyl, Diarrheasaurus, Itchybuttosaurus, Stink Kong, Great Woolly Butthead, and Tyrannosore-arse Rex. And as if all this wasn't bad enough, it's also full of truly disgusting facts about buttolution, primitive butteria, famarse buttosaurologists, the exstinktion of the buttosaurs, and the history of the univarse.

If you are shocked, confused, frightened, or offended by any — or all — of these things (which, of course, you are because you are an adult), please put the book down immediately and go find something more suitable for a grown-up. Like a book on car insurance, for instance. Or the history of golf. Or a home-decorating guide.

If, on the other hand, you find yourself vaguely amused, slightly curious, or even excited by any — or all — of the things that you have just been warned about, then by all means be our guest and read the book . . . Just don't say that you weren't warned.

The Publishers

WHAT BUTTOSAUR IS THAT?

ANDY GRIFFITHS

ILLUSTRATED BY TERRY DENTON

Scholastic Inc.

New York   Toronto   London   Auckland   Sydney
Mexico City   New Delhi   Hong Kong   Buenos Aires

CONTENTS

Introduction

Life on Earth began with primitive butteria that appeared in the oceans during the Pre-Crappian era 600 million years ago. Over time, these butteria buttvolved into more complex forms of butt life, including invertebutts, buttfish, buttphibians, stenchtiles, farthropods, stinksects, and buttornithids, until eventually giving rise to the group of stenchtiles we know as the buttosaurs.

Buttosaurs appeared on Earth 203 million years ago at the beginning of the Triarssic period. They came in a stunning variety of shapes and sizes, with an equally stunning variety of stinks and stenches.

Dominating butt life on Earth for the next 150 million years, buttosaurs disappeared from the fossil record around 65 million years ago. The exstinktion of the buttosaurs allowed a new species of butt life, called bummals, to buttvolve, eventually leading to the emergence of the earliest butt-men.

Although the focus of this book is on buttosaurs, examples of butt-related life-forms from all major groups have been included in order to provide the most comprehensive and up-to-date guide to prehistoric butt life ever published.

Buttfish Sea Scorpibuns Spiny Butt-urchin Octoste
corpibuns Spiny Butt-urchin Octostenchosaurus Butt-sp
ctostenchosaurus Butt-sponge Trilobutt Jelly Buttfish
ctostenchosaurus Butt-sponge Trilobutt Jelly Buttfish Sea S
utt-sponge Trilobutt Jelly Buttfish Sea Scorpibuns Spiny
lly Buttfish Sea Scorpibuns Spiny Butt-urchin Octostenchos
corpibuns Spiny Butt-urchin Octostenchosaurus Butt-sp
ctostenchosaurus Butt-sponge Trilobutt Jelly Buttfish
ctostenchosaurus Butt-sponge Trilobutt Jelly Buttfish Sea S
utt-sponge Trilobutt Jelly Buttfish Sea Scorpibuns Spiny
lly Buttfish Sea Scorpibuns Spiny Butt-urchin Octostench
corpibuns Spiny Butt-urchin Octostenchosaurus Butt-sp
ctostenchosaurus Butt-sponge Trilobutt Jelly Buttfish
ctostenchosaurus Butt-sponge Trilobutt Jelly Buttfish Sea S
utt-sponge Trilobutt Jelly Buttfish Sea Scorpibuns Spiny
lly Buttfish Sea Scorpibuns Spiny Butt-urchin Octostench
corpibuns Spiny Butt-urchin Octostenchosaurus Butt-sp
ctostenchosaurus Butt-sponge Trilobutt Jelly Buttfish Sea S
ctostenchosaurus Butt-sponge Trilobutt Jelly Buttfish
utt-sponge Trilobutt Jelly Buttfish Sea Scorpibuns Spiny B
lly Buttfish Sea Scorpibuns Spiny Butt-urchin Octostench
corpibuns Spiny Butt-urchin Octostenchosaurus Butt-sp
ctostenchosaurus Butt-sponge Trilobutt Jelly Buttfish
ctostenchosaurus Butt-sponge Trilobutt Jelly Buttfish Sea S
tt-sponge Trilobutt Jelly Buttfish Sea Scorpibuns Spiny
ly Buttfish Sea Scorpibuns Spiny Butt-urchin Octostench
corpibuns Spiny Butt-urchin Octostenchosaurus Butt-sp
ctostenchosaurus Butt-sponge Trilobutt Jelly Buttfish Sea S
ctostenchosaurus Butt-sponge Trilobutt Jelly Buttfish
utt-sponge Trilobutt Jelly Buttfish Sea Scorpibuns Spiny
lly Buttfish Sea Scorpibuns Spiny Butt-urchin Octostench

Invertebutts

Life on Earth began in the seas with primitive
butteria during the Pre-Crappian era. Over time,
these early single-cheeked butts clumped together
to form some of the first multi-cheeked invertebutts
in the Crapozoic era oceans.

BUTT-SPONGE
TRILOBUTT
JELLY BUTTFISH
SEA SCORPIBUNS
SPINY BUTT-URCHIN
OCTOBUTTOPUS

Butt-sponge

The Butt-sponge lived permanently attached to the sea floor, absorbing butteria. It had two distinct cheeks, which is the identifying characteristic of all forms of butt life, both modern and prehistoric.

What it lacked, however, were arms, legs, a mouth, internal organs, a nervous system, a personality, and hobbies or interests of any kind.

It is believed that the species was forced to buttvolve other features, such as the ability to create bubbles by releasing gas underwater, in an effort to entertain itself and relieve the boredom of its incredibly dull life.

VITAL STATISTICS

Scientific name: *Squeezius cheeki*
Family: Squisherbutt
Diet: Butteria-ivorarse
Time: Crappian 540–500 million years ago
Stink rating:

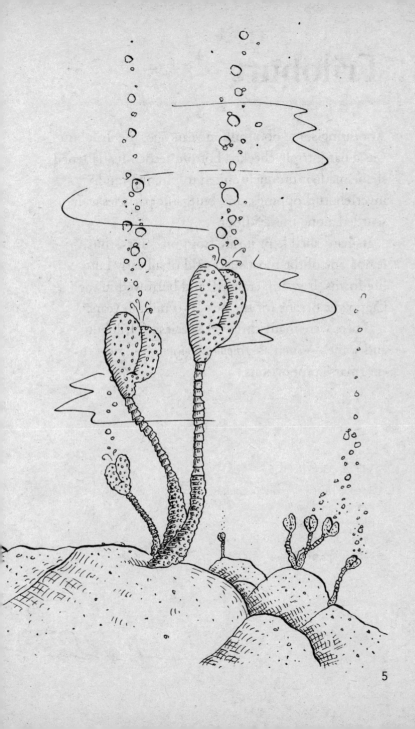

Trilobutt

Appearing some 600 million years ago, the Trilobutt was a hard, triple-cheeked bottom feeder. Its flattened shape made it uniquely suited to filtering mud, invertebutt droppings, and buttganic particles as it scuttled along the sea floor.

Its hard shell kept it safe from predators; thus, it was one of the most successful of all early butt life-forms. It swam, crawled, and burrowed in the Crapozoic oceans for the next 350 million years.

There were many different species of Trilobutt, and some — such as *Trilobuttus gigantis* — grew to enormarse proportions.

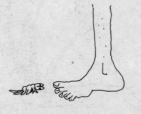

VITAL STATISTICS

Scientific name: *Tricheekium buttus*
Family: Stinkerbutt
Diet: Mudivorarse
Time: Crapozoic era 540–250 mya
Stink rating: 🐾🐾🐾🐾🐾

Jelly Buttfish

Despite having no bones, no heart, no blood, and no brains, the gas-filled, buttcheek-shaped Jelly Buttfish was one of the fiercest of the later soft-bodied invertebutts.

Jelly Buttfish traveled in large schools, trailing their long stenchtacles behind them. These stenchtacles each had a deadly jelly-butt on the end, which could swiftly kill captured prey by infecting it with deadly butteria. The Jelly Buttfish would then absorb the prey's body by buttosis, a primitive form of osmosis in which food is absorbed through tiny pores in the butt cheeks.

VITAL STATISTICS

Scientific name: *Piscatis jellibulus*
Family: Squisherbutt
Diet: Carnivorarse
Time: Ordungocian 500–435 mya
Stink rating:

Sea Scorpibuns

The Sea Scorpibuns was the giant ancestor of the modern-day scorpion, and one of the most feared prehistoric deep-water butt life-forms. The enormous claws of a Sea Scorpibuns could cut a giant Trilobutt in half, and the venom sacs in its butt-shaped stinger contained raw sewage so potent that it could kill a school of Jelly Buttfish within seconds.

Evidence suggests, however, that these terrifying creatures engaged in quite elegant courtship rituals. These would begin with the male grasping the female's pincers and performing a dance called the *buttenade de deux*. This dance eventually developed into a range of styles, including buttroom dancing, butt-ballet, stench-jazz, and stink-hop.

VITAL STATISTICS

Scientific name: *Scorpius oceania*
Family: Pinchabutt
Diet: Carnivorarse
Time: Ordungocian, Sewerian 500–410 mya
Stink rating: 💩💩

Spiny Butt-urchin

One of the spikiest and most unpleasant of the unpleasant prehistoric deep-water creatures, the Spiny Butt-urchin left behind a trail of death and destruction wherever it went.

Although it fed exclusively on other smaller Spiny Butt-urchins (stuffing them two or three at a time into its horrid little spiny mouth), many other creatures were spiked to death on its long spiny spines as it moved across the prehistoric ocean floor in search of more Spiny Butt-urchins to stuff into its horrid little spiny mouth.

VITAL STATISTICS

Scientific name: *Spinius butti*
Family: Cannibalobutt
Diet: Spiny butt-urchinivorarse
Time: Ordungocian 500–435 mya
Stink rating: 🌸🌸🌸🌸🌸

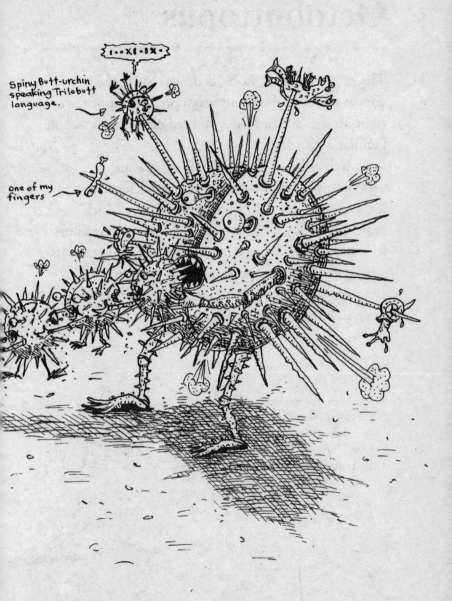

Octobuttopus

The eight-armed, eight-headed, sixteen-cheeked, sixteen-eyed Octobuttopus was a predecessor of the eight-armed, one-headed, two-eyed octopus that we are familiar with today.

As well as being bizarre in appearance, the Octobuttopus had a highly developed defense system. If threatened, it would eject eight clouds of thick brownish liquid to blind — and disgust — predators. It would then use the incredible thrusting power of its sixteen cheeks to escape at high speed, leaving its attacker completely grossed out and in desperate need of an industrial-strength disinfectant.

VITAL STATISTICS

Scientific name: *Octavio posteriosi*
Family: Freakasaur
Diet: Carnivorarse
Time: Sewerian 435–410 mya
Stink rating:

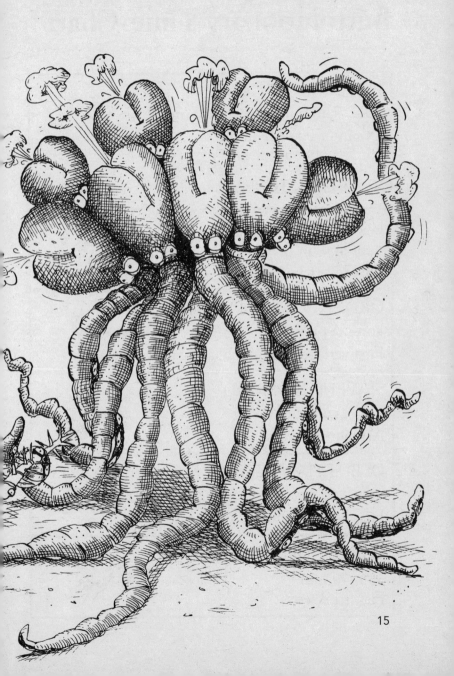

15

Buttolutionary Time-Chart

PRE-CRAPPIAN TIME
4600–540 million years ago (mya)
Origin of butt life in the sea

CRAPOZOIC ERA

CRAPPIAN PERIOD
540–500 mya
First invertebutts

ORDUNGOCIAN PERIOD
500–435 mya
First vertebutts (buttfish) and butt-plants

SEWERIAN PERIOD
435–410 mya
Armoured buttfish

DEBUTTIAN PERIOD
410–355 mya
First buttphibians

CARBUTTIFEROUS PERIOD
355–295 mya
First stinksects

POOMIAN PERIOD
First stenchtiles
295–250 mya

MESSOZOIC ERA

TRIARSSIC PERIOD
First buttosaurs
250–203 mya

JURARSSIC PERIOD
First flying buttosaurs
203–135 mya

CRAPACEOUS PERIOD
135–65 mya
First gigantic buttosaurs

SCENTOZOIC ERA

FARTOCENE EPOCH
65–1.75 mya
First bummals

BUMOCENE EPOCH
1.75 mya–present
First Buttanderthals and butt-men

ish Colonacanth Buttray Stinkleosteus Butt-head Sl
uttray Stinkleosteus Butt-head Shark Deep-sea
tinkleosteus Butt-head Shark Deep-sea Butt-dangle
utt-head Shark Deep-sea Butt-dangler Brown-blobpe
Deep-sea Butt-dangler Brown-blobpedo Fish Colonacant
rown-blobpedo Fish Colonacanth Buttray Stinkleost
ish Colonacanth Buttray Stinkleosteus Butt-he
Colonacanth Buttray Stinkleosteus Butt-head Shark
uttray Stinkleosteus Butt-head Shark Deep-sea
tinkleosteus Butt-head Shark Deep-sea Butt-dangle
utt-head Shark Deep-sea Butt-dangler Brown-blobpe
Deep-sea Butt-dangler Brown-blobpedo Fish Colonacant
rown-blobpedo Fish Colonacanth Buttray Stinkleos
ish Colonacanth Buttray Stinkleosteus Butt-he
Colonacanth Buttray Stinkleosteus Butt-head Shark
uttray Stinkleosteus Butt-head Shark Deep-sea
tinkleosteus Butt-head Shark Deep-sea Butt-dangle
utt-head Shark Deep-sea Butt-dangler Brown-blobpe
Deep-sea Butt-dangler Brown-blobpedo Fish Colonacant
rown-blobpedo Fish Colonacanth Buttray Stinkleos
ish Colonacanth Buttray Stinkleosteus Butt-he
olonacanth Buttray Stinkleosteus Butt-head Shark
uttray Stinkleosteus Butt-head Shark Deep-sea
tinkleosteus Butt-head Shark Deep-sea Butt-dangle
utt-head Shark Deep-sea Butt-dangler Brown-blobpe
Deep-sea Butt-dangler Brown-blobpedo Fish Colonacant
rown-blobpedo Fish Colonacanth Buttray Stinkleost
ish Colonacanth Buttray Stinkleosteus Butt-he
olonacanth Buttray Stinkleosteus Butt-head Shark
uttray Stinkleosteus Butt-head Shark Deep-sea

Buttfish

Major advances in buttolution during the Crapozoic era saw the rise of the first vertebutts (butt life-forms with internal skeletons). During the Ordungocian period (500–435 million years ago), the first buttfish appeared and soon buttvolved into an astonishing variety of forms that quickly came to dominate the prehistoric seas.

BROWN-BLOBPEDO FISH

COLONACANTH

BUTTRAY

STINKLEOSTEUS

BUTT-HEAD SHARK

DEEP-SEA BUTT-DANGLER

Brown-blobpedo Fish

The Brown-blobpedo Fish was one of the earliest butt life-forms to use brown blobs — self-propelled, cigar-shaped missiles — as a means of attack and defense.

The Brown-blobpedo Fish launched these brown blobs, or blobpedoes, at any creature unfortunate enough to stray into its territory, usually with predictably devarsetating results.

Successive generations of Brown-blobpedo Fish developed the ability to equip their blobpedoes with homing devices and explosive heads. The Brown-blobpedo Fish eventually became exstinkt because its blobpedoes achieved such explosive power that they often detonated on launch and buttbliterated the Brown-blobpedo Fish itself.

VITAL STATISTICS

Scientific name: *Blobpedis rancidius*
Family: Crapofish
Diet: Needle Kelpivorarse
Time: Ordungocian, Sewerian 500–410 mya
Stink rating: ✿✿✿✿✿

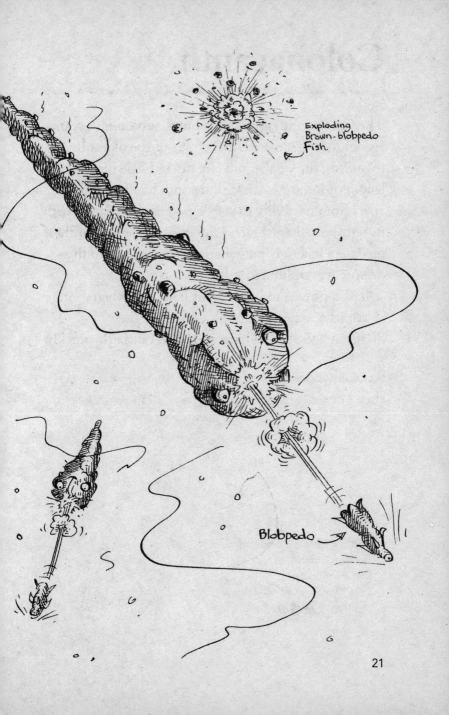

Exploding
Brown-blobpedo
Fish.

Blobpedo →

Colonacanth

The Colonacanth appeared around 400 million years ago and was a close relative of one of the oldest living fossil fish, the Coelacanth (see inset). Little more than a length of intestine, the Colonacanth had few defenses apart from its ability to startle potential predators with its ugly butt-shaped face. Unfortunately, many of these predators had ugly butt-shaped faces as well, so this defense was of limited value.

It also proved to be a serious handicap when trying to attract a mate. As a result of both of these disadvantages, the Colonacanth died out fairly quickly.

VITAL STATISTICS

Scientific name: *Colonic contagium*
Family: Ickyafish
Diet: Pooivorarse
Time: Ordungocian 500–435 mya
Stink rating:

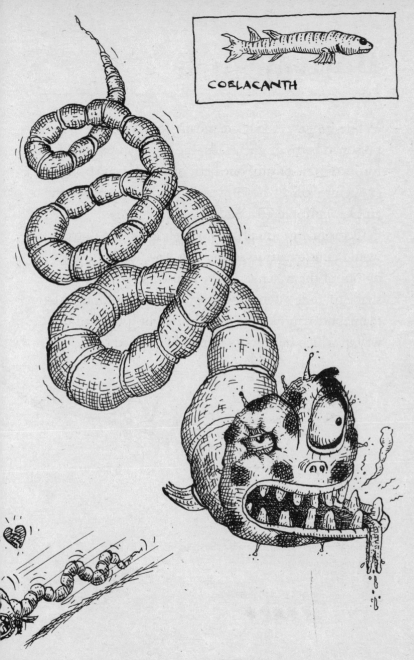

COELACANTH

Buttray

While stingrays today are mostly feared for the poisoned barbs on their tails, the Buttray was feared for its terrible breath, one blast of which was strong enough to kill a whole forest of needle kelp or reduce an Octobuttopus to a puddle of brown jelly.

Occasionally, usually when frightened, the Buttray would emit breath so strong that it would blast itself up out of the water and have to use its aerobuttnamic shape to glide safely back down again. It is thought by many buttosaurologists that this might have been one way in which buttosaurs eventually learned to fly.

Razor-
sharp
barbs

VITAL STATISTICS

Scientific name: *Halitosis horrendous*
Family: Stenchafish
Diet: Herbivorarse
Time: Sewerian 435–410 mya
Stink rating: 🌑🌑🌑🌑🌑

Buttray using bad breath to blast itself out of water

Extremely
foul breath

Stinkleosteus

Stinkleosteus was enormarse, and one of the first armored buttfish to evolve. Its bony plating protected it from the powerful pincers of such predators as the Sea Scorpibuns, and also shielded it against the withering effects of the Buttray's lethally smelly breath. Its third eye proved to be of great benefit in spotting — and thus avoiding — the deadly brown blobs fired by the Brown-blobpedo Fish.

An undisputed ruler of the oceans, the enormarse, heavily armored Stinkleosteus thrived throughout the Sewerian period.

VITAL STATISTICS

Scientific name: *Stinki indestructiblus*
Family: Squisherfish
Diet: Omnivorarse
Time: Sewerian 435–410 mya
Stink rating: 🌸🌸🌸🌸🌸

Bony
plating

Deadly brown
blobpedo

Butt-head Shark

A close relative of the better-known — and still existing — Hammerhead Shark, the Butt-head Shark suffered from very low self-esteem due to the fact that everyone called it a butt-head. Which was true, but nonetheless very hurtful. For instance, how would you like it if everybody called *you* a butt-head? It would be hurtful enough even if you didn't have a butt-head, but imagine how much more it would hurt if you did.

It was perhaps the hurtful nature of this taunt that accounted for the extraordinary frequency and severity of Butt-head Shark attacks during the Carbuttiferous period.

So the Butt-head Shark teaches us an important lesson: Be kind to others . . . even if they act like butt-heads, and especially if they do have a butt-shaped head.

VITAL STATISTICS

Scientific name: *Butt-headius maximus*
Family: Buttshark
Diet: Carnivorarse
Time: Carbuttiferous 355–295 mya
Stink rating: ✿✿✿✿✿

29

Deep-sea Butt-dangler

The Deep-sea Butt-dangler got its name from the bioluminescent butt that dangled from its dorsal spine. Millions of light-producing buteria caused this false butt to glow a blue-green color. These colorful lures came in a variety of styles, and no two were the same. Some had flashing pimples; others had warts capable of impressive strobe-lighting effects.

The Deep-sea Butt-dangler used its false butt to attract prey. It would wiggle the false butt in front of its large, fang-packed mouth. Then, when its fascinated, almost hypnotized, prey moved close enough, the Deep-sea Butt-dangler would flick its dangling butt out of the way and snap up the prey in its powerful jaws.

VITAL STATISTICS

Scientific name: *Dangleri prosthetica*
Family: Freakafish
Diet: Buttfishivorarse
Time: Carbumiferous 355–295 mya
Stink rating: ✿✿✿✿✿✿

Buttolution: How Life Buttvolved

Life on Earth began with butteria that appeared in the oceans 600 million years ago. Over time, these butteria buttvolved into more complex forms of butt life until eventually giving rise to the group of stenchtiles we know as the buttosaurs. The exstinktion of the buttosaurs around 65 million years ago allowed a new species of butt life, called bummals, to buttvolve, eventually leading to the emergence of the earliest butt-men.

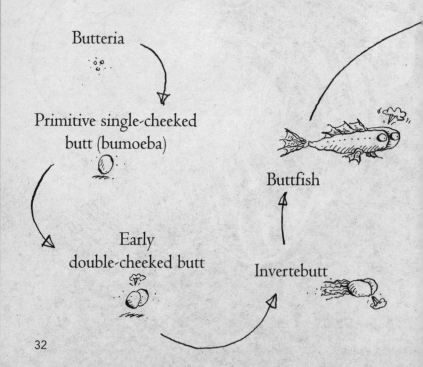

Butteria

Primitive single-cheeked butt (bumoeba)

Early double-cheeked butt

Invertebutt

Buttfish

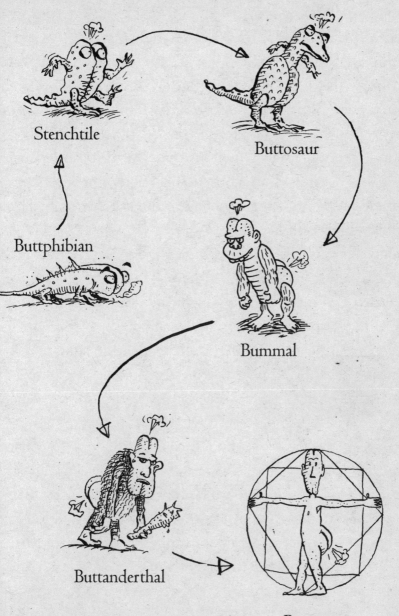

Stenchtile

Buttosaur

Buttphibian

Bummal

Buttanderthal

Butt-man

33

utteuodon Poopigator Dungosaurus Turdle Buttaconstric
ungosaurus Turdle Buttaconstrictor Buttskipper Bogasaurus
uttaconstrictor Buttskipper Bogasaurus Buttetrodon
uttskipper Bogasaurus Buttetrodon Poopigator Dungosaurus
uttetrodon Poopigator Dungosaurus Turdle Buttaconstric
ungosaurus Turdle Buttaconstrictor Buttskipper Bogasau
uttaconstrictor Buttskipper Bogasaurus Buttetrodon Poopi
uttskipper Bogasaurus Buttetrodon Poopigator Dungosa
uttetrodon Poopigator Dungosaurus Turdle Buttaconstric
ungosaurus Turdle Buttaconstrictor Buttskipper Bogasau
uttaconstrictor Buttskipper Bogasaurus Buttetrodon Poopi
uttskipper Bogasaurus Buttetrodon Poopigator Dungosa
uttetrodon Poopigator Dungosaurus Turdle Buttaconstric
ungosaurus Turdle Buttaconstrictor Buttskipper Bogasau
uttaconstrictor Buttskipper Bogasaurus Buttetrodon Poopi
uttskipper Bogasaurus Buttetrodon Poopigator Dungosaurus
uttetrodon Poopigator Dungosaurus Turdle Buttaconstric
ungosaurus Turdle Buttaconstrictor Buttskipper Bogasaurus B
uttaconstrictor Buttskipper Bogasaurus Buttetrodon Poopi
uttskipper Bogasaurus Buttetrodon Poopigator Dungosaurus
uttetrodon Poopigator Dungosaurus Turdle Buttaconstric
ungosaurus Turdle Buttaconstrictor Buttskipper Bogasau
uttaconstrictor Buttskipper Bogasaurus Buttetrodon Poopi
uttskipper Bogasaurus Buttetrodon Poopigator Dungosa
uttetrodon Poopigator Dungosaurus Turdle Buttaconstric
ungosaurus Turdle Buttaconstrictor Buttskipper Bogasaurus B
uttaconstrictor Buttskipper Bogasaurus Buttetrodon
uttskipper Bogasaurus Buttetrodon Poopigator Dungosaurus
uttetrodon Poopigator Dungosaurus Turdle Buttaconstric
ungosaurus Turdle Buttaconstrictor Buttskipper Bogasaurus B
uttaconstrictor Buttskipper Bogasaurus Buttetrodon

Buttphibians & Stenchtiles

Around 400 million years ago, using their fins as
primitive limbs, some of the more adventurous
buttfish crawled onto land to take up residence in
the abundant swamps and bogs of the Crapozoic
era. The descendants of these brave pooineers
buttvolved into the first buttphibians
and stenchtiles.

BUTTSKIPPER

BOGASAURUS

BUTTETRODON

POOPIGATOR

DUNGOSAURUS

TURDLE

BUTTACONSTRICTOR

Buttskipper

The Buttskipper was one of the first true buttphibians, able to live both in and out of the water. On land, the Buttskipper moved along the bog shores by "skipping" on its butt-shaped fins.

   Living on land gave the Buttskipper tremendous advantages, the most important of which was the ability to release gas in private without the embarrassing telltale bubbles that accompany it in water. Of course, releasing gas above water meant the noises that often accompany the action could be heard clearly for the first time. These noises, however, were deemed so amusing that the Buttskipper was happy to give up its recently won privacy, and rapidly developed the full range of expressive sound effects that butts still employ — and enjoy so much — today.

VITAL STATISTICS

Scientific name: *Tetratis poddus*
Family: Stinkophibian
Diet: Herbivorarse
Time: Debuttian 410–355 mya
Stink rating:

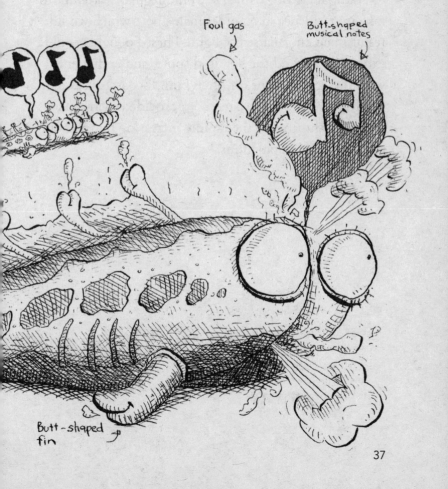

Foul gas

Butt-shaped musical notes

Butt-shaped fin

Bogasaurus

The Bogasaurus, as its name suggests, was generally found in a bog. These huge, brown, particularly foul-smelling bogs were created by the male Bogasaurus in order to attract a female, known as a Bogasauress.

Young male Bogasauruses would regularly attempt to take up residence in an older male's bog, which would result in an enormarse bogfight. These bogfights could extend far beyond the bog in dispute, and ended only with the death of one, or often both, Bogasauruses.

Meanwhile, their vacated bogs provided living space and nourishment for the rapidly increasing buttphibian and stenchtile populations.

VITAL STATISTICS

Scientific name: *Bogassius bogi*
Family: Crapophibian
Diet: Bogivorarse
Time: Carbuttiferous 355–295 mya
Stink rating: ✿ ✿ ✿ ✿ ✿

Buttetrodon

Buttetrodon featured a butt-shaped "sail" rising from its back. This sail was made up of ten hollow spines covered in thick pink skin.

There is much speculation about the purpose of this sail. Some buttosaurologists think that the hollow spines served as "chimneys," which helped to release the excess gases caused by the Buttetrodon's exclusive diet of stinkants.

Other buttosaurologists believe that the Buttetrodon's sail was intended to make its butt appear much bigger than it actually was in order to scare away predators.

VITAL STATISTICS

Scientific name: *Buttus sailius*
Family: Stinkotile
Diet: Stinkantivorarse
Time: Poomian 295–250 mya
Stink rating: 🐾🐾🐾🐾🐾

Poopigator

The Poopigator bore a strong resemblance to the modern alligator, only it was much bigger, much browner, and much, much smellier. While its appearance was quite threatening, the Poopigator's breath was far worse than its bite. Nevertheless, its bite was still quite bad.

The Poopigator consumed large prey by dragging it into a bog and then spinning or convulsing wildly until bite-size pieces were torn off. This is referred to as the "deathbog roll" — not to be confused with "bog roll," which is Australian slang for toilet paper.

VITAL STATISTICS

Scientific name: *Poopius gatori*
Family: Crapotile
Diet: Omnivorarse
Time: Poomian 295–250 mya
Stink rating: 🐾🐾🐾🐾

Dungosaurus

Dungosaurus was one of the earliest stenchtiles to appear on Earth. These large lizardlike creatures had tough, scaly skins that stopped their cheeks from drying out. They were therefore able to live exclusively on land.

Stenchtiles were so named because their diet consisted mainly of bog, which gave them their distinctive — and very strong — "stench."

Dungosaurus made the most of this feature by using its stench as a means of defense. If threatened, it would inflate its expandable cheek sacs to ten times their normal size and then release an overpowering cloud of foul-smelling odor.

These cheek displays also may have been used by males in courting rituals, the odor in this case serving as a primitive perfume irresistible to the female Dungosaurus.

VITAL STATISTICS

Scientific name: *Scatius maximius*
Family: Stinkotile
Diet: Bogivorarse
Time: Poomian 295–250 mya
Stink rating: 🐾🐾🐾🐾🐾

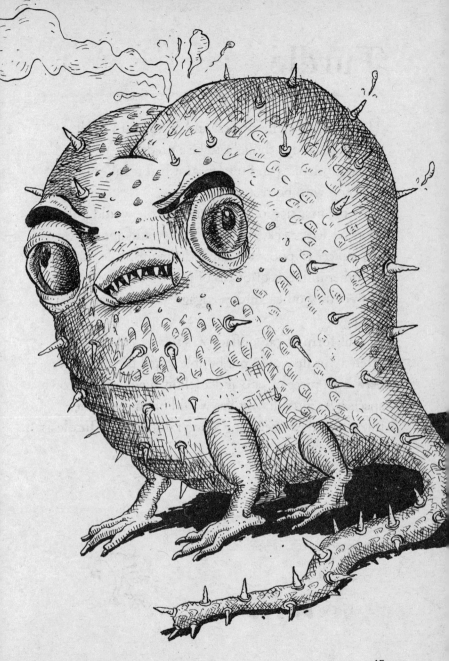

Turdle

The Turdle was the slowest and most timid of all stenchtiles and is thought to be a predecessor of modern tortoises and turtles, as it had features in common with both species.

At the first sign of danger, the Turdle would pull in its arms, legs, neck, and head so it would appear to be just a piece of poo, virtually indistinguishable from all the other millions of pieces of poo on the ground . . . or were they other Turdles engaged in a similar defense strategy?

This form of camouflage was so successful that often a Turdle would not be able to tell the difference between a piece of poo and a fellow member of its own species. As a result, Turdles would often make the tragic mistake of selecting a poo rather than a Turdle as a lifetime partner.

VITAL STATISTICS

Scientific name: *Turdi domesticus*
Family: Turdotile
Diet: Herbivorarse
Time: Triarssic 250–203 mya
Stink rating: 🐾🐾🐾🐾

Buttaconstrictor

Easily the longest of all known stenchtiles, the Buttaconstrictor lived a dreary and unpleasant life, dragging its super-stretched buttocks through the bog and dung that covered 99.99999% of the Earth's surface during the Messozoic era.

A brutal hunter, the Buttaconstrictor liked to wrap its extraordinarily elongated cheeks around its victim and squeeze it to death before swallowing it whole.

One of the Buttaconstrictor's favorite foods was the Toiletbrushasaurus, and it was capable of devouring a complete herd of these hardworking creatures during a single hunt. Unfortunately, the Buttaconstrictor's Toiletbrushasaurus binges only served to worsen the condition of the prehistoric buttvironment and make things even more unpleasant for itself.

VITAL STATISTICS

Scientific name: *Lengthius cheeki*
Family: Freakatile
Diet: Toiletbrushasauruses
Time: Messozoic 135–65 mya
Stink rating: ✿✿✿✿✿

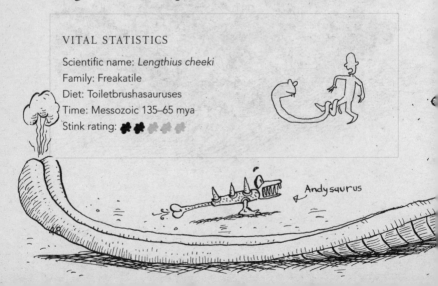

Andysaurus

Prehistoric Butt-plant Life

The first plants appeared in the abundant warm cracks and bogs of the Ordungocian period. By the end of the Debuttian, plants were flourishing in almost every habitat on Earth and were every bit as rich, varied, and smelly as the butt-related life-forms that fed on them.

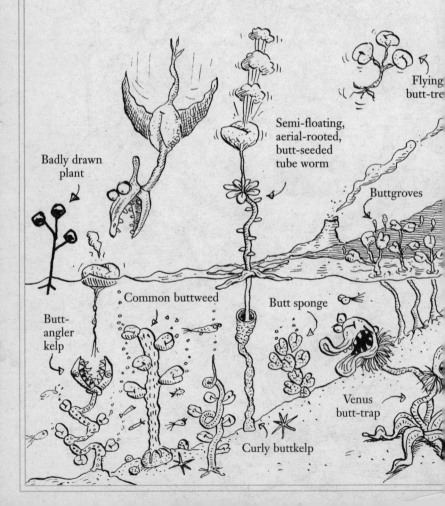

Flying butt-tre

Semi-floating, aerial-rooted, butt-seeded tube worm

Badly drawn plant

Buttgroves

Common buttweed

Butt sponge

Butt-angler kelp

Venus butt-trap

Curly buttkelp

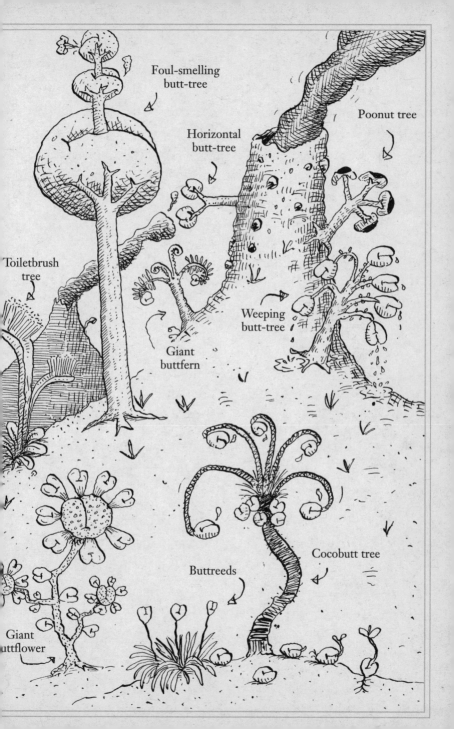

uttsquito Giant Mutant Blowfly Buttantula Giant Pr
Mutant Blowfly Buttantula Giant Prehistoric Stinkant
uttantula Giant Prehistoric Stinkant Buttipede Buttslu
rehistoric Stinkant Buttipede Buttslug Buttsquito G
uttipede Buttslug Buttsquito Giant Mutant Blowfly Bu
uttsquito Giant Mutant Blowfly Buttantula Giant Pr
Mutant Blowfly Buttantula Giant Prehistoric Stinkant
uttantula Giant Prehistoric Stinkant Buttipede Buttslu
rehistoric Stinkant Buttipede Buttslug Buttsquito G
uttipede Buttslug Buttsquito Giant Mutant Blowfly Bu
uttsquito Giant Mutant Blowfly Buttantula Giant Pr
Mutant Blowfly Buttantula Giant Prehistoric Stinkant
uttantula Giant Prehistoric Stinkant Buttipede Buttslu
rehistoric Stinkant Buttipede Buttslug Buttsquito G
uttipede Buttslug Buttsquito Giant Mutant Blowfly Bu
uttsquito Giant Mutant Blowfly Buttantula Giant Pr
Mutant Blowfly Buttantula Giant Prehistoric Stinkant
uttantula Giant Prehistoric Stinkant Buttipede Buttslu
rehistoric Stinkant Buttipede Buttslug Buttsquito Giant
uttipede Buttslug Buttsquito Giant Mutant Blowfly Bu
uttsquito Giant Mutant Blowfly Buttantula Giant Prehisto
Mutant Blowfly Buttantula Giant Prehistoric Stinkant
uttantula Giant Prehistoric Stinkant Buttipede Buttslug B
rehistoric Stinkant Buttipede Buttslug Buttsquito Giant
uttipede Buttslug Buttsquito Giant Mutant Blowfly Bu
uttsquito Giant Mutant Blowfly Buttantula Giant Pr
Mutant Blowfly Buttantula Giant Prehistoric Stinkant
uttantula Giant Prehistoric Stinkant Buttipede Buttslug B
rehistoric Stinkant Buttipede Buttslug Buttsquito C
uttipede Buttslug Buttsquito Giant Mutant Blowfly Bu

Farthropods & Stinksects

Hot on the heels of the buttphibians, sea-dwelling invertebutts rapidly buttvolved their own creeping, crawling, flying, and farting armies to invade the land.

BUTTIPEDE

BUTTSLUG

BUTTSQUITO

GIANT MUTANT BLOWFLY

BUTTANTULA

GIANT PREHISTORIC STINKANT

Buttipede

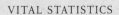

An early relative of the millipede and centipede families, the Buttipede had 2,000 legs and 1,000 butts, which made it very slow and very smelly. However, it was a strong burrower and its thousand-butt power made it very good at converting buttganic matter into rich bumus (or humus), a medium vital to the growth of healthy plants. The speed at which the Buttipede did this ensured the continuance of the cycle of fertility and, by extension, all buttosaur and butt-related life on Earth.

Unfortunately, the job of keeping its many butts clean was difficult for the Buttipede — its body was so long and so far behind that it was often in a different year, or in some extreme cases, a completely different century.

VITAL STATISTICS

Scientific name: *Millibuttus leggus*
Family: Nauseopod
Diet: Dirtivorarse
Time: Carbuttiferous 355–295 mya
Stink rating: 💨💨

Slimey
decayed
cocobutt

Buttslug

Truly deserving of its place in the Disgustapod family, the Buttslug did little but froth and burp and swear and gurgle and bubble and slime its way through the prehistoric landscape without so much as an "excuse me" or a "thank you." Now, to be fair, the buttosaur world was hardly a place for fancy manners, but even so, the Buttslug really was outrageous. If another butt creature was foolish enough to get between the Buttslug and a can of Buttslug Cola, it would simply unleash a torrent of slimy mucarse and drown the unfortunate animal.

VITAL STATISTICS

Scientific name: *Frothus revolti*
Family: Disgustapod
Diet: Buttslug Colavorarse
Time: Carbuttiferous 355–295 mya
Stink rating:

Buttsquito

The Buttsquito was similar to the modern mosquito, only much bigger, with many species growing to be the size of a light aircraft. Also, unlike mosquitoes today, which will feed on any exposed part of a victim's body, the Buttsquito would attack only the butt of its prey. And a Buttsquito bite did not just leave a small, itchy, red bump on the victim's skin, either. In fact, a Buttsquito's victim often didn't have any skin left at all. Or flesh. Or blood. Or bones. Because the larger species of Buttsquito had the ability to suck its victim's entire body up through its enormarse buttboscis.

VITAL STATISTICS

Scientific name: *Buttboscius massiosius*
Family: Horribilosect
Diet: Butt-bloodivorarse
Time: Carbuttiferous 355–295 mya
Stink rating: 🦨

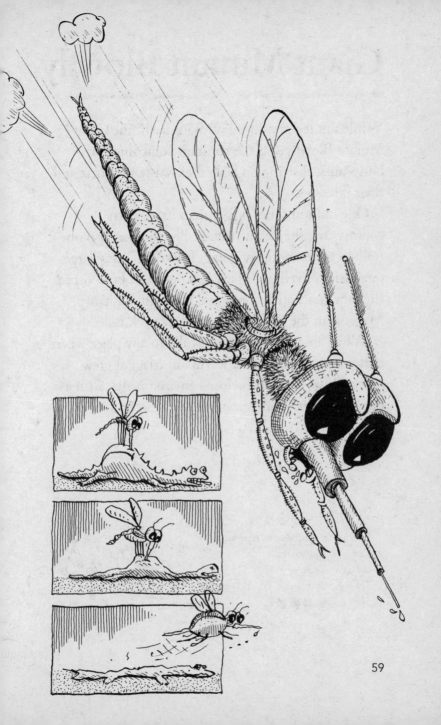

59

Giant Mutant Blowfly

While not technically a buttosaur itself, the Giant Mutant Blowfly was the constant companion of buttosaurs, thriving on both their waste products and their carcasses.

One million times bigger than its modern counterpart, the Giant Mutant Blowfly was also one million times more annoying. It liked to spray large quantities of yellowy-green goo out of its buttboscis, suck the head off its prey, and lay Giant Mutant Maggots in the unfortunate victim's neck-hole.

While able to adapt successfully to any place where buttosaurs lived, the Giant Mutant Maggot grew especially gigantic in enclosed environments, such as buttcanoes and underground caves (also known as maggotoriums).

VITAL STATISTICS

Scientific name: *Mutatis blowflyus*
Family: Disgustosect
Diet: Omnivorarse
Time: Carbuttiferous 355–295 mya
Stink rating: 🖤🖤🖤

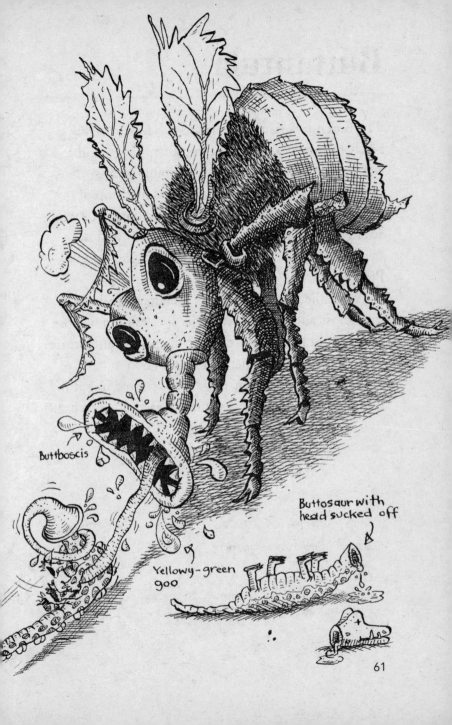

Buttboscis

Buttosaur with
head sucked off

Yellowy-green
goo

61

Buttantula

The Buttantula had an enormarse abdobutt, eight beady brown eyes, two terrifying sharp fangs, and eight powerful legs. The butt-web built by this prehistoric, spiderlike Freakapod was made up of long brown strands of butt silk. These butt-webs were strong enough to catch large stinksects, as well as flying buttosaurs, such as Buttadactyls and Pteranobutts.

While the Buttantula remained largely unchanged for almost 200 million years, the species did not exist in large numbers due to the fact that most Buttantulas were scared of each other. And with good reason — attempts at mating often resulted in both Buttantulas crushing and stenching each other to death.

VITAL STATISTICS

Scientific name: *Posterius terribulus*
Family: Freakapod
Diet: Carnivorarse
Time: Triarssic, Jurarssic, Crapaceous 250–65 mya
Stink rating: 🌸🌸🌸

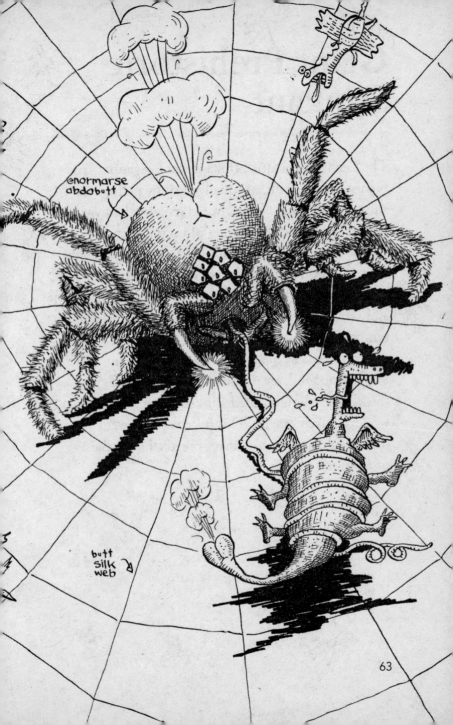

enormarse
abdabutt

butt
silk
web

63

Giant Prehistoric Stinkant

The Giant Prehistoric Stinkant was a gigantic prehistoric ant with an equally gigantic prehistoric stink. It was generally bright red in color, had vicious pincers, and lived in colonies of up to 200,000.

The Giant Prehistoric Stinkant was highly sought after as a food source by some buttosaurs because eating the ant would usually result in terrible flatulence and serious body odor, which helped to increase a buttosaur's status in any herd's gassing order.

If squashed by a larger buttosaur, the Giant Prehistoric Stinkant produced huge quantities of a thick, greasy liquid called stinkant juice, which was excessively smelly. This juice was the exclusive diet of the Microbuttosaurus, one of the smelliest of all buttosaurs.

VITAL STATISTICS

Scientific name: *Stinkantius giganti*
Family: Rancidosect
Diet: Carnivorarse
Time: Triarssic, Jurarssic, Crapaceous 250–65 mya
Stink rating: ✿ ✿ ✿ ✿ ✿

How a Buttosaur Works

From the outside, buttosaurs may have appeared to be little more than unpleasant loads of blubber, gas, and brown blobs.
The truth is, however, that they were highly complex loads of blubber, gas, and brown blobs, as the following cutaway diagram clearly demonstrates.

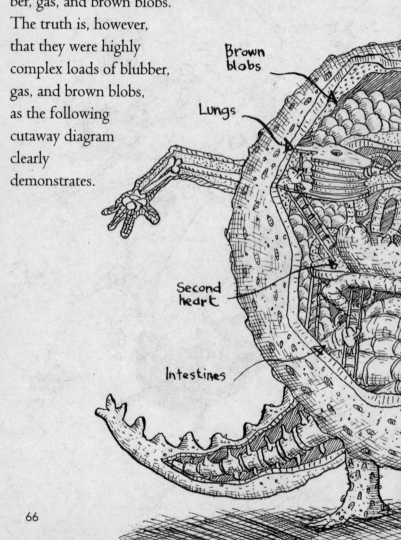

Brown blobs

Lungs

Second heart

Intestines

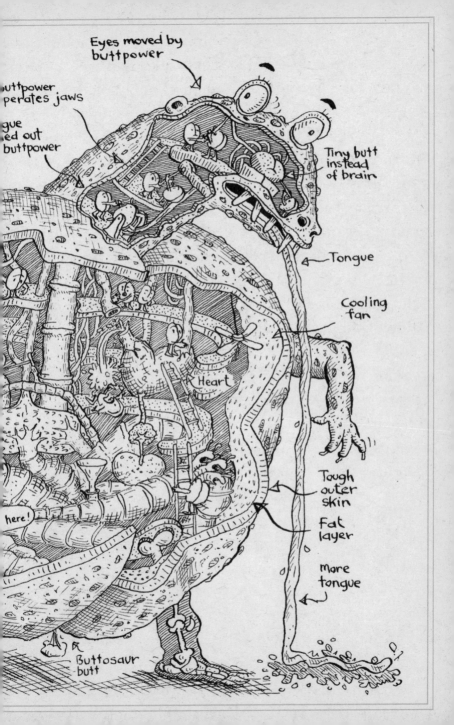

Eyes moved by
buttpower

uttpower
perates jaws

gue
ed out
buttpower

Tiny butt
instead
of brain

Tongue

Cooling
fan

Heart

here!

Tough
outer
skin

Fat
layer

more
tongue

Buttosaur
butt

iapersaurus Diarrheasaurus Itchybuttosaurus Lace-collared Cy
ink Kong Toiletbrushasaurus Tricerabutt Tyrannosore-arse
uttosaurus Microbuttosaurus Stenchgantorsaurus Poopasaur
iotasaurus The Very Rare Long-necked Long-legged Sho
iotasaurus Butt-eyed Buttosaurus Buttontopinus Diapers
clopootops Skullbuttosaurus Sparebuttosaurus Stink Kong
gbuttosaurus Gigantabuttosaurus Great White Buttosauru
iletrollasaurus Badlydrawn Buttosaurus Butt-headed Idio
upid-looking Tiny Butt-headed Droopy-eyed Idiotasaurus
iapersaurus Diarrheasaurus Itchybuttosaurus Lace-collared C
ink Kong Toiletbrushasaurus Tricerabutt Tyrannosore-arse
uttosaurus Microbuttosaurus Stenchgantorsaurus Poopasaur
iotasaurus The Very Rare Long-necked Long-legged Sho
iotasaurus Butt-eyed Buttosaurus Buttontopinus Diaper
clopootops Skullbuttosaurus Sparebuttosaurus Stink Kong
gbuttosaurus Gigantabuttosaurus Great White Buttosaurt
iletrollasaurus Badlydrawn Buttosaurus Butt-headed Idic
upid-looking Tiny Butt-headed Droopy-eyed Idiotasaurus
iapersaurus Diarrheasaurus Itchybuttosaurus Lace-collared Cy
ink Kong Toiletbrushasaurus Tricerabutt Tyrannosore-arse
uttosaurus Microbuttosaurus Stenchgantorsaurus Poopasaur
iotasaurus The Very Rare Long-necked Long-legged Sho
iotasaurus Butt-eyed Buttosaurus Buttontopinus Diapers
clopootops Skullbuttosaurus Sparebuttosaurus Stink Kong
gbuttosaurus Gigantabuttosaurus Great White Buttosaurt
iletrollasaurus Badlydrawn Buttosaurus Butt-headed Idiotas
upid-looking Tiny Butt-headed Droopy-eyed Idiotasaurus
iapersaurus Diarrheasaurus Itchybuttosaurus Lace-collared Cy
ink Kong Toiletbrushasaurus Tricerabutt Tyrannosore-arse
uttosaurus Microbuttosaurus Stenchgantorsaurus Poopasaur

Buttosaurs

The Messozoic era saw the rise of some of the most well known, most aggressive, and most stupid members of the buttosaur family.

POOPASAUR
TOILETROLLASAURUS
BADLYDRAWN BUTTOSAURUS
BUTT-HEADED IDIOTASAURUS
VERY RARE LONG-NECKED LONG-LEGGED
SHORT-TAILED STUPID-LOOKING TINY
BUTT-HEADED DROOPY-EYED IDIOTASAURUS
BUTT-EYED BUTTOSAURUS
BUTTONTOPIMUS
DIAPERSAURUS
DIARRHEASAURUS
ITCHYBUTTOSAURUS
LACE-COLLARED CYCLOPOOTOPS
SKULLBUTTOSAURUS
SPAREBUTTOSAURUS
STINK KONG
TOILETBRUSHASAURUS
TRICERABUTT
TYRANNOSORE-ARSE REX
BIGBUTTOSAURUS
GIGANTABUTTOSAURUS
GREAT WHITE BUTTOSAURUS
MICROBUTTOSAURUS
STENCHGANTORSAURUS

Poopasaur

The Poopasaur had brown skin, an enormarse mouth, small black eyes, sharp teeth, very bad breath, and an even worse temper. It was well camouflaged for life in the swamps and primeval cocobutt-tree forests and was prone to hiding in the undergrowth and then jumping out unexpectedly to catch its prey, which it would swallow in one gulp.

Unfortunately, its enormarse mouth was much bigger than its stomach, and the Poopasaur would often overeat until it exploded.

The deadly brown clouds caused by these explosions — known as "brown-outs" — made it impossible for other buttosaurs to see or breathe, and could last for several hours.

VITAL STATISTICS

Scientific name: *Crocodilius crappius*
Family: Craposaur
Diet: Omnivorarse
Time: Messozoic 250–65 mya
Stink rating:

Exploding
poopasaur →

Toiletrollasaurus

The Toiletrollasaurus appeared in a dazzling variety of colors, patterns, and textures. The various subspecies differed immensely in size, weight, tear-ability, softness, "finger-breakthrough" resistance, and degrees of absorption.

Despite these differences, they shared one common feature: a permanent expression of terror due to the fact that they were preyed upon by almost every other type of buttosaur. The Toiletrollasaurus was widely hunted because it was prized for its long, soft, absorbent tail. It is thought that the perforations on the Toiletrollasaurus's tail buttvolved as a defense against its many predators. Like some species of modern-day lizard, if caught by the tail, it could lose a section and then regrow it.

VITAL STATISTICS

Scientific name: *Papyrus posteri*
Family: Wipeosaur
Diet: Herbivorarse
Time: Poomian 295–250 mya
Stink rating: 🦠

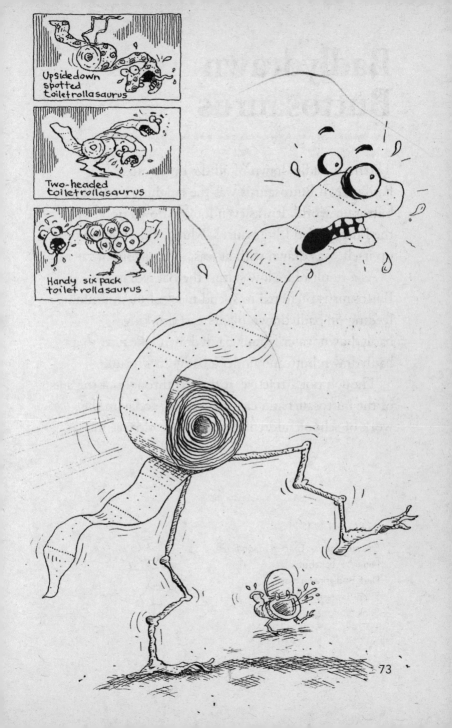

Upsidedown
spotted
toiletrollasaurus

Two-headed
toiletrollasaurus

Handy six pack
toilet rollasaurus

Badlydrawn Buttosaurus

The most badly drawn of all the buttosaurs, Badlydrawn Buttosaurus was the laughingstock of the buttosaur world. It was even looked down upon by the Butt-headed Idiotasaurus, which, although no pin-up itself, was drawn with at least a modicum of talent.

As a result of its low status, the Badlydrawn Buttosaurus preferred to spend most of its time alone, feeding on badlydrawn plants and drinking badlydrawn water from a badlydrawn lake next to a badlydrawn buttcano under a badlydrawn sun.

Though not attractive, it thrived throughout the age of the buttosaurs and can still be seen today in the work of schoolchildren all over the world (see inset).

VITAL STATISTICS

Scientific name: *Craperi magnificus*
Family: Freakabutt
Diet: Badlydrawn plants
Time: Triarssic 250–203 mya
Stink rating: 🌸🌸🌸🌸🌸

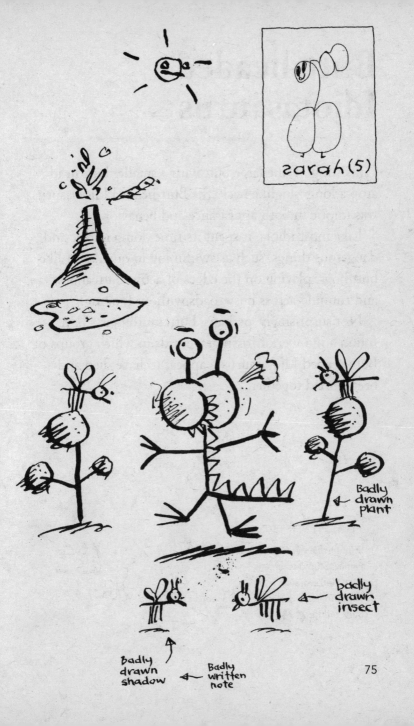

sarah (5)

Badly
drawn
plant

Badly
drawn
insect

Badly
drawn
shadow

Badly
written
note

75

Butt-headed Idiotasaurus

Consisting of one large butt with a smaller butt-head atop a long, sluglike neck, the Butt-headed Idiotasaurus was idiotic in both appearance and behavior.

Like most idiots, it spent its time doing idiotic and dangerous things, such as swimming in quicksand-like butt-bogs, playing on the edges of active buttcanoes, and running across busy roads without looking.

Not surprisingly, perhaps, buttosaurologists have found a number of fossil graveyards in which groups of Butt-headed Idiotasauruses appear to have died and been buried together.

VITAL STATISTICS

Scientific name: *Dumbuttius minor*
Family: Stupidosaur
Diet: Herbivorarse
Time: Triarssic, Jurarssic, Crapaceous 250–65 mya
Stink rating: 💩💩💩💩💩

Very Rare Long-necked Long-legged Short-tailed Stupid-looking Tiny Butt-headed Droopy-eyed Idiotasaurus

The Very Rare Long-necked Long-legged Short-tailed Stupid-looking Tiny Butt-headed Droopy-eyed Idiotasaurus was very rare due to the fact that it was too stupid to eat, drink, find shelter, or even mate. If it did manage to reproduce, it was usually by accident.

In fact, the only interesting fact about the Very Rare Long-necked Long-legged Short-tailed Stupid-looking Tiny Butt-headed Droopy-eyed Idiotasaurus is that it had the longest and stupidest-sounding name of all the buttosaurs.

VITAL STATISTICS

Scientific name: *Dumbuttius major*
Family: Stupidosaur
Diet: Too dumb to eat
Time: Triarssic 250–203 mya
Stink rating: 🌸🌸🌸🌸🌸

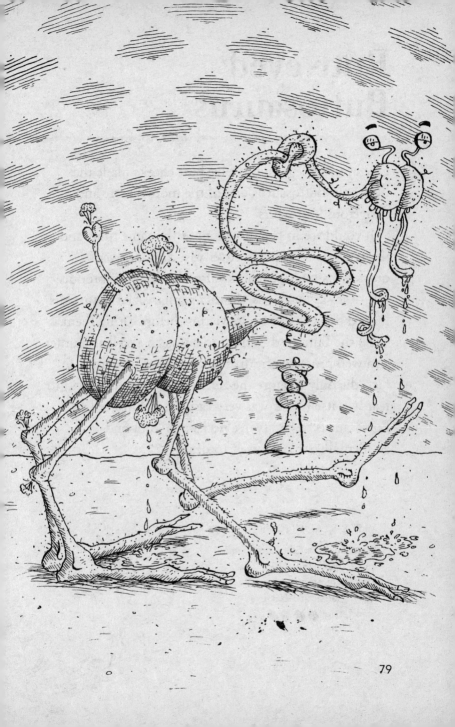

Butt-eyed Buttosaurus

Five eyes, six legs, and twelve butt cheeks made the Butt-eyed Buttosaurus one of the more bizarre and dangerous buttosaurs.

It could see in five directions at the same time, and its six legs allowed it to cover vast distances very quickly. Its multiple cheeks also allowed it to produce five times as much gas as other similar-sized buttosaurs. It used this gas to stun its victims before eating them.

So the Butt-eyed Buttosaurus was an excellent hunter and well protected from attack by other predators. In fact, the only creature the Butt-eyed Buttosaurus had to fear was itself, as it was very easy for a Butt-eyed Buttosaurus to get its five necks in a knot and accidentally strangle itself to death.

VITAL STATISTICS

Scientific name: *Stupido stupendius*
Family: Freakabutt
Diet: Carnivorarse
Time: Triarssic 250–203 mya
Stink rating: 🍀🍀🍀🍀

Buttontopimus

Buttontopimus spent most of its time stumbling around holding its "head," trying to think of what to do next. This, of course, was impossible because its "head" was in fact a butt and as such it had no brain. The lack of a brain meant that it also had no memory, thus it often forgot that it had no brain, which is why it continued to spend so much of its time holding its "head" and trying to think.

The sheer stupidity of the Buttontopimus made it an obvious target for any buttosaur looking for an easy meal, and thus the species sadly became exstinkt quite soon after it first appeared. Not that it really mattered — Buttontopimuses were too stupid to know that they had even existed in the first place.

VITAL STATISTICS

Scientific name: *Butterius cranium*
Family: Stupidosaur
Diet: Can't remember to eat
Time: Triarssic 250–203 mya
Stink rating:

Diapersaurus

Coming in two main species, Cloth and Disposable, the small, highly intelligent Diapersaurus would attach itself to a newborn buttosaur of another species. This arrangement was beneficial to both parties. The Diapersaurus was provided with nourishment and protection from other large buttosaurs, and the young buttosaur was protected from the harsh conditions of the prehistoric buttosaur world.

These relationships were usually short-term, however, as the baby buttosaur would eventually outgrow the Diapersaurus and shed it, much like a snake sheds its skin. If it belonged to the Cloth species, the Diapersaurus would then move on and find a new host. If it belonged to the Disposable species, the Diapersaurus would die as soon as it was discarded.

Diapersaurus attaches itself to a newborn buttosaur.

Mature buttosaur shedding its Diapersaurus.

VITAL STATISTICS

Scientific name: *Pantus putridi*
Family: Stinkosaur
Diet: Pooivorarse
Time: Triarssic 250–203 mya
Stink rating: 🌼🌼🌼🌼🌼

Diarrheasaurus

Extremely unpleasant in both appearance and odor, the Diarrheasaurus also had one of the most unpleasant life cycles of all buttosaurs.

Due to its runny consistency, Diarrheasaurus was unable to pick itself up off the ground and seek shelter from the hot Triarssic sun. This meant that it was usually baked hard within hours of being born and mistaken for a crunchy snack by an unsuspecting buttosaur. After eating the toxic Diarrheasaurus, this buttosaur would suffer horrible stomach pains, increased gas, and terrible diarrhea. Soon after, the Diarrheasaurus would be expelled from the sick buttosaur's body and deposited on the ground in its liquid form once more — ready to start its life cycle over again.

VITAL STATISTICS

Scientific name: *Puddle detestabilis*
Family: Craposaur
Diet: Unknown
Time: Triarssic 250–203 mya
Stink rating: ✿✿✿✿✿

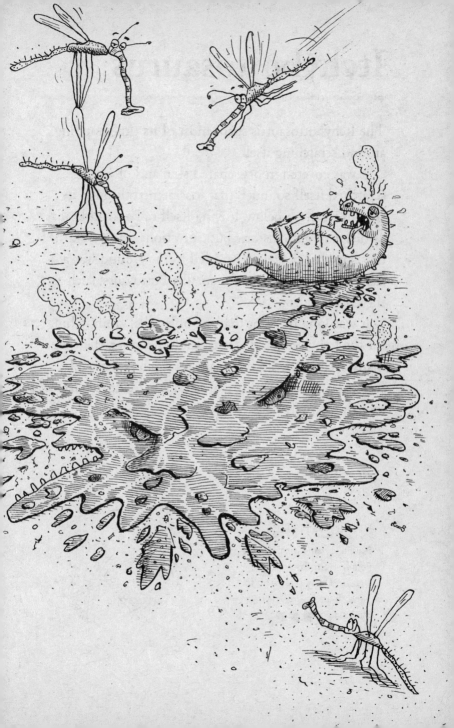

Itchybuttosaurus

The Itchybuttosaurus spent most of its time hopping around scratching itself.

It was covered in dry, chafed skin and often scratched itself so much that it scratched through its skin to the flesh below, leaving itself open to all kinds of disgusting prehistoric butt infections. However, the dry skin that flaked off and fell to the ground was a rich source of nutrients for smaller buttosaurs, such as the Diapersaurus.

It was long thought that the only relief from itching for the Itchybuttosaurus was death; however, there are many accounts from buttosaur museum curators of reconstructed Itchybuttosaurus bones attempting to scratch themselves.

VITAL STATISTICS

Scientific name: *Itchi itchisori*
Family: Horribilosaur
Diet: Too busy scratching to eat
Time: Triarssic 250–203 mya
Stink rating: ♣♣♣♣♣

Lace-collared Cyclopootops

Named after Cyclops, the legendary one-eyed giant, the Lace-collared Cyclopootops was the most glamorous member of the buttosaur family. Its huge lacy collar was both a defense mechanism — making it appear larger than it actually was — and a prehistoric fashion statement.

With its long curling eyelashes, rounded cheeks, and painted toenails, the Lace-collared Cyclopootops had a sense of beauty and style way ahead of its time. Fashionologists trace the popularity of lace collars in the 16th and 17th centuries directly back to this creature.

Although it died out with the rest of the buttosaurs at the end of the Crapaceous period, the Lace-collared Cyclopootops nevertheless has been admired by many cults throughout the last 65 million years.

VITAL STATISTICS

Scientific name: *Cyclopius amazingus*
Family: Freakabutt
Diet: Fashion magazines
Time: Jurarssic, Crapaceous 203–65 mya
Stink rating: 💩💩💩💩💩

Pointy
things

Skullbuttosaurus

The Skullbuttosaurus was a nocturnal buttosaur, and when it wasn't engaged in violent skull-butting contests with rival Skullbuttosauruses, it could usually be found stalking the cocobutt forests at night and using its alarming appearance to scare its prey to death. At the approach of a Skullbuttosaurus, other buttosaurs would spontaneously evacuate themselves or simply drop dead with fright.

Even gigantosaurs, such as the Bigbuttosaurus and the Gigantabuttosaurus, were scared of the Skullbuttosaurus. As a result, the Skullbuttosaurus always had an abundant food supply and became very widespread by the end of the Crapaceous period.

VITAL STATISTICS

Scientific name: *Cranium enormi*
Family: Horribilosaur
Diet: Carnivorarse
Time: Jurarssic, Crapaceous 203–65 mya
Stink rating: ✿ ✿ ✿ ✿ ✿

Sparebuttosaurus

A passive and comparatively peaceful buttosaur, the Sparebuttosaurus gets its name from the row of miniature butts sticking up from its neck, back, and tail. It is thought that these butts allowed the Sparebuttosaurus to replace itself in the event of a fatal accident or attack.

If a Sparebuttosaurus was killed, then any of the undamaged "spare" butts could detach themselves and grow to become exact, fully formed replicas of the dead Sparebuttosaurus. If any of these new Sparebuttosauruses were killed, too, then their spare butts could grow into perfect replicas and so on, effectively making the Sparebuttosaurus virtually indestructible.

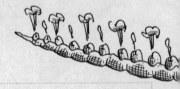

VITAL STATISTICS

Scientific name: *Replicus arsius*
Family: Stenchosaur
Diet: Herbivorarse
Time: Jurarssic, Crapaceous 203–65 mya
Stink rating: 🌸🌸🌸

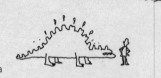

Rebirth of a
Sparebuttosqurus

ture
e

Stink Kong

This huge, gorilla-like buttosaur was covered in fur except for two bare patches on the front of each of its cheeks. These were caused by its habit of pounding on itself with its fists to produce a terrifying booming sound. This pounding also served to activate its numerous stench glands to produce a terrifying stink, hence its name.

Though resembling a gorilla in appearance, Stink Kong had little else in common with the herbivorarse, herd-dwelling ape. Stink Kong was a clumsy, stupid, aggressive loner who liked nothing better than to get involved in violent brawls with any buttosaur willing to take it on. It and the Great White Buttosaurus were natural enemies and often engaged in ferocious battles that lasted for many hours.

VITAL STATISTICS

Scientific name: *Fragrantus regis*
Family: Stinkosaur
Diet: Omnivorarse
Time: Jurarssic, Crapaceous 203–65 mya
Stink rating: ✿✿✿✿✿

Toiletbrushasaurus

The Toiletbrushasaurus was the toilet cleaner of the prehistoric buttosaur world. Not that "toilets" actually existed at the time, which is exactly why the Toiletbrushasaurus played such a vital role in prehistoric Earth's ecology.

Always in a hurry, the Toiletbrushasaurus moved quickly. As it did so, its many strong bristly legs swept, cleaned, and cleared the ground so that the rest of the buttosaurs actually had somewhere to walk instead of having to slosh around in their own . . . well, let's just say that the average buttosaur produced up to 40 pounds of it a day . . . and there were a lot of buttosaurs . . . which is probably why the Toiletbrushasaurus was always in such a hurry.

VITAL STATISTICS

Scientific name: *Bristilus lavatorum*
Family: Eeeuuw!osaur
Diet: Pooivorarse
Time: Messozoic 250-65 mya
Stink rating: 🐾🐾🐾🐾🐾

Tricerabutt

The Tricerabutt was a triple-cheeked buttosaur with bony armor plating and tusk-like wart-horns growing out of each of its cheeks.

Tricerabutts tended to form gangs of three, which would then spend most of their time running around looking for other gangs of Tricerabutts to attack and stab with their horns. Drive-by hornings were common, despite the fact that cars were not to be invented for at least another 65 million years.

The Tricerabutt was not overly bright. Fossilized Tricerabutt bones show that many Tricerabutts died after running into trees, getting their horns stuck, and not being able to get them out again.

VITAL STATISTICS

Scientific name: *Tricerabuttius*
Family: Stupidosaur
Diet: Herbivorarse
Time: Jurarssic 203–135 mya
Stink rating: 🐾🐾🐾🐾🐾

Tyrannosore-arse Rex

There were few buttosaurs with a worse temper than the Tyrannosore-arse Rex. Driven into wild rages by the pain in its gigantic aching cheeks, it would rampage through the prehistoric forest, leaving hundreds of other buttosaurs either gassed, brown-blobbified, or completely flattened.

The funny thing — or not so funny if you happened to be a Tyrannosore-arse Rex — was that these rampages only served to make it even sorer — and angrier — than before.

Some experts blame the Tyrannosore-arse Rex and its destructive rages for the exstinktion of many species of small buttosaurs. Others just feel sorry for it. Only one thing is known for sure: Tyrannosore-arse Rex had a really sore behind.

VITAL STATISTICS

Scientific name: *Soreius cheekius*
Family: Terribilosaur
Diet: Omnivorarse
Time: Jurarssic 203–135 mya
Stink rating: 💩💩💩💩💩

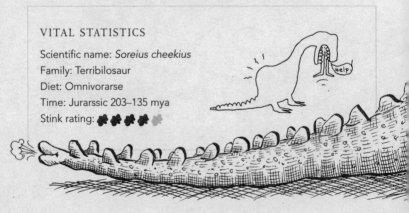

Bigbuttosaurus

The Bigbuttosaurus was so named because of its incredibly big rear end. It was so big that every time Bigbuttosaurus sat down, it killed at least five other smaller buttosaurs. Despite this, it was a gentle but clumsy giant that lived on the juicy leaves and cocobutts from the tops of cocobutt trees.

The rear end of the Bigbuttosaurus continued to expand to increasingly alarming proportions throughout the Crapaceous period, and some buttosaurologists believe that the exstinktion of the buttosaurs was due to the Bigbuttosauruses' big butts becoming so big that they blotted out the sun and plunged the Earth into an extended big-butt–induced winter.

VITAL STATISTICS

Scientific name: *Superio humungarse*
Family: Gigantosaur
Diet: Herbivorarse
Time: Crapaceous 135–65 mya
Stink rating: ♣ ♣ ♣ ♣ ♣

Gigantabuttosaurus

The largest of all of the buttosaurs, the
Gigantabuttosaurus was only on Earth for a
comparatively brief time. The creature was
so heavy that when it walked it created giant
cracks in the ground into which it would
often fall. The stupid little arms and feeble
little legs of the Gigantabuttosaurus were
of no use for climbing, so any that fell
would then perish in these self-created
"cracks of doom."

VITAL STATISTICS

Scientific name: *Superius gigantus*
Family: Gigantosaur
Diet: Omnivorarse
Time: Crapaceous 135–65 mya
Stink rating: ✿✿✿✿✿

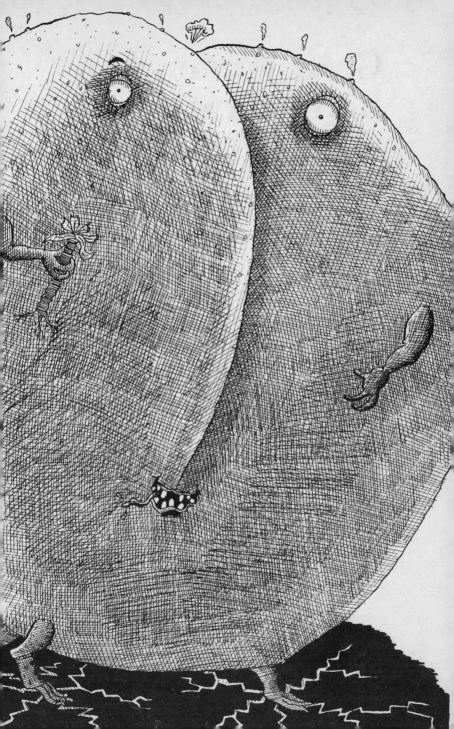

Great White Buttosaurus

The Great White Buttosaurus appeared on Earth toward the late Crapaceous era. One of the truly gigantic buttosaurs, its most distinctive feature was its blindingly white skin. It is thought that this bioluminescence gave it a great advantage when fighting, as its incredible brightness could temporarily blind an opponent.

Some believe that the expression "he/she thinks that the sun shines out of his/her behind" dates from the time that buttosaurologists first discovered fossil evidence of the Great White Buttosaurus.

The Great White Buttosaurus was also well known for its habit of dumping gigantic brown blobs on top of its enemies.

VITAL STATISTICS

Scientific name: *Maximus albinus*
Family: Disgustosaur
Diet: Omnivorarse
Time: Crapaceous 135–65 mya
Stink rating: 🐾 🐾 🐾 🐾 🐾

Microbuttosaurus

The Microbuttosaurus was the smallest of all known buttosaurs, but it is classed as belonging to the Gigantosaur family because of its massively putrid, nostril-burning, nausea-inducing, eyebrow-singeing, throat-gagging, lung-collapsing, migraine-making, fever-causing, heart-stopping, blood-curdling, eyeball-popping stink.

With this stink, which is thought to have been caused by its exclusive diet of stinkant juice, it was capable of knocking out — and sometimes even killing — buttosaurs up to 100,000 times its size.

Small in stature, the Microbuttosaurus was nevertheless enormous in impact. Some experts even speculate that the exstinktion of the buttosaurs may have been caused by a sudden explosion in the Microbuttosaurus population.

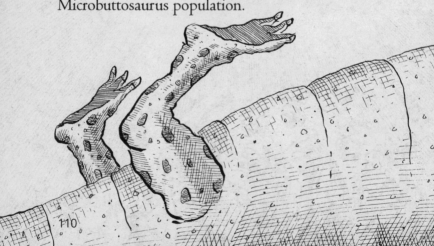

Scientific name: *Pongius maximus*
Family: Gigantosaur
Diet: Stinkant-juiceivorarse
Time: Crapaceous 135–65 mya
Stink rating:

Stenchgantorsaurus

The Stenchgantorsaurus was one of the ugliest, dirtiest, wartiest, pimpliest, grossest, greasiest, hairiest, and stinkiest of all the buttosaurs.

It is thought that it grew to be so disgusting because it lived such a long life — some specimens have been found that are thought to have had a life span of at least 400 years. And 400 years is a long time for a butt to go without being wiped. As a result, the Stenchgantorsaurus was completely blind, and was one of the few buttosaurs to have a highly developed sense of smell, which it used to locate prey.

It was also prone to developing enormarse butt-pimples, which would often burst in spectacular fashion, similar in force and devarsetation to a buttcano eruption.

VITAL STATISTICS

Scientific name: *Stenchus gantori*
Family: Stenchosaur
Diet: Omnivorarse
Time: Crapaceous 135–65 mya
Stink rating: 💩💩💩💩💩

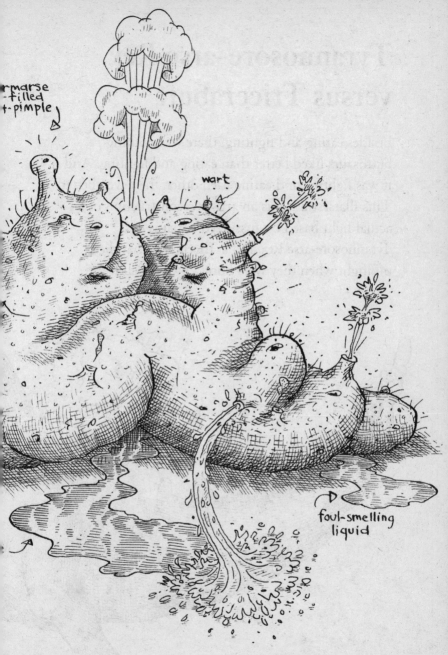

marse
-filled
t-pimple

wart

foul-smelling
liquid

Tyrannosore-arse Rex versus Tricerabutt

Besides eating and fighting, there was nothing buttosaurs liked better than eating and fighting. And if it was fighting and eating each other, then even better. This illarsestration is an artist's reconstruction of an actual fight based on fossilized remains of a Tyrannosore-arse Rex and a Tricerabutt that died midfight when they were buried by a bogslide.

ni Buttosaurus Buttadactyl Arseyopteryx Fartosaurus
ni Buttosaurus Buttadactyl Arseyopteryx Farto
gh-speed Mini Buttosaurus Buttadactyl Ars
derpantsosaurus High-speed Mini Buttosaurus
ranobutt Underpantsosaurus High-speed Mini Bu
x Pteranobutt Underpantsosaurus High-speed
shasaurus Rex Pteranobutt Underpantsosaurus
tosaurus Flushasaurus Rex Pteranobutt Under
eyopteryx Fartosaurus Flushasaurus Rex Pterar
tadactyl Arseyopteryx Fartosaurus Flushasaurus
tosaurus Buttadactyl Arseyopteryx Fartosaurus Fl
ni Buttosaurus Buttadactyl Arseyopteryx Fartosaurus
ni Buttosaurus Buttadactyl Arseyopteryx Fartos
gh-speed Mini Buttosaurus Buttadactyl Ars
derpantsosaurus High-speed Mini Buttosaurus
ranobutt Underpantsosaurus High-speed Mini Bu
x Pteranobutt Underpantsosaurus High-speed
shasaurus Rex Pteranobutt Underpantsosaurus
tosaurus Flushasaurus Rex Pteranobutt Under
eyopteryx Fartosaurus Flushasaurus Rex Pterar
tadactyl Arseyopteryx Fartosaurus Flushasaurus
tosaurus Buttadactyl Arseyopteryx Fartosaurus Fl
ni Buttosaurus Buttadactyl Arseyopteryx Fartosaurus
ni Buttosaurus Buttadactyl Arseyopteryx Fartos
gh-speed Mini Buttosaurus Buttadactyl Ars
derpantsosaurus High-speed Mini Buttosaurus
ranobutt Underpantsosaurus High-speed Mini Bu
x Pteranobutt Underpantsosaurus High-speed
shasaurus Rex Pteranobutt Underpantsosaurus
tosaurus Flushasaurus Rex Pteranobutt Under

Buttornithids

As competition on the land became ever more intense, some of the buttosaurs began to take advantage of the thrusting power of their gas emissions and launched themselves into the air. Others supplemented their gas power with large saggy flaps of skin, which they used as primitive wings, and gradually learned to master controlled flight.

BUTTADACTYL

ARSEYOPTERYX

FARTOSAURUS

FLUSHASAURUS REX

PTERANOBUTT

UNDERPANTSOSAURUS

HIGH-SPEED MINI BUTTOSAURUS

Buttadactyl

The Buttadactyl was one of the first butts to take to the air. It had a vast wingspan, but its "wings" were actually nothing more than large, loose, leathery flaps of buttcheek skin, and it gained most of its lift and speed from its abundant gas power.

Unfortunately, the Buttadactyl was at the mercy of its primitive, crudely formed bowels and would often go out of control like a balloon that is blown up and then let go without its end being tied.

Clogging the skies during the late Triarssic period, Buttadactyls were largely responsible for the creation of the methane layer in the Earth's atmosphere.

VITAL STATISTICS

Scientific name: *Cheekum flaparsius*
Family: Flapposaurid
Diet: Carnivorarse
Time: Triarssic 250–203 mya
Stink rating: 🍀 🍀 🍀 🍀 🍀

Buttadactyl flies out of control after gas explosion

Arseyopteryx

Arseyopteryx was the world's first true flying butt, as opposed to butts that just accidentally blasted themselves into the air as a result of unexpectedly violent emissions.

While Arseyopteryx certainly relied on the same basic thrusting power, it is thought that its ability to control its flight might have developed as a result of its having dry, flaky skin. The large, scale-like pieces of dry skin covering Arseyopteryx eventually became so pronounced that they formed the first primitive butt feathers, which in turn formed the first true wings.

As time went on, Arseyopteryx developed more flying skill and progressed from simple solo joy flights to being able to impress potential mates by putting on spectacular hot-air shows.

VITAL STATISTICS

Scientific name: *Plumae ridiculus*
Family: Arsornithine
Diet: Bum-seedivorarse
Time: Jurarssic 203–135 mya
Stink rating: 🔥🔥🔥

Fartosaurus

The Fartosaurus was a unique creature — a buttosaur that was formed from the floating gases of several other species of buttosaur. While the Fartosaurus lived a relatively peaceful life compared to other buttosaurs, it could, however, be extremely dangerous. It was capable of descending on its prey and smothering it whole in a silent but deadly manner.

Although it had no natural predators, the greatest threat to the Fartosaurus came from the natural elements. A Fartosaurus could easily be broken up and dissipated by strong winds, and due to its highly flammable nature would often burst into flames when struck by lightning.

VITAL STATISTICS

Scientific name: *Stinkius vaporarse*
Family: Gasornithid
Diet: Carnivorarse
Time: Jurarssic 203–135 mya
Stink rating: ✿✿✿✿

123

Flushasaurus Rex

The Flushasaurus Rex was not an ancient predecessor of the modern flush toilet, as is often thought. In fact, despite sharing the same basic shape, they are not related at all.

The Flushasaurus Rex had wings, legs, and a barbed tail. Modern flush toilets have none of these. Another major difference is that the Flushasaurus Rex did not dispose of waste like a modern toilet, but instead spent most of its time hurling great loads of dirty, smelly water out of its mouth. This was done in self-defense, as other buttosaurs were always trying to sit on it, which was probably due to the extreme shortage of modern flush toilets on Earth during the reign of the buttosaurs.

VITAL STATISTICS

Scientific name: *Vomitus projectilius*
Family: Freakasaurid
Diet: Carnivorarse
Time: Jurarssic 203–135 mya
Stink rating:

125

Pteranobutt

The Pteranobutt was one of the fiercest of the flying buttosaurs. It spent most of its time flying around and knocking other smaller flying buttosaurs out of the sky with the thick bony butt attached to the end of its whiplike tail.

As the Pteranobutt was herbivorarse, this behavior was not motivated so much by the need for food as by the fact that it was just a bully that liked picking on flying buttosaurs smaller than itself.

By the end of the Jurarssic period, the other buttosaurs had had enough of Pteranobutt's bullying, and they would regularly gang up to take their revenge on one by pushing its head into the mouth of a Flushasaurus Rex.

VITAL STATISTICS

Scientific name: *Whackius grandis*
Family: Whackornithid
Diet: Herbivorarse
Time: Jurarssic 203–135 mya
Stink rating: ✿✿✿✿✿

Flushasaurus
rex

127

Underpantsosaurus

Underpantsosauruses mostly traveled in pairs, though they sometimes formed large groups known as multipacks. These multipacks sometimes contained so many Underpantsosauruses that they would form a cloud thick enough to block out the sun. Events such as these struck fear into the hearts of land-dwelling buttosaurs, which could imagine nothing worse than being trapped inside a big dirty stinky smelly pair of Underpantsosauruses.

Unlike most buttosaurs, the Underpantsosaurus did not die out completely, but rather buttvolved over many millions of years, becoming gradually smaller and more fashionable. During this process of buttolution, the Underpantsosaurus lost its ability to fly, and the more modern species were eventually domesticated by butt-men and kept in underwear drawers.

VITAL STATISTICS

Scientific name: *Jockus maximus*
Family: Knickersaurid
Diet: Carnivorarse
Time: Jurarssic 203–135 mya
Stink rating: 🐾🐾🐾🐾🐾

High-speed Mini Buttosaurus

The High-speed Mini Buttosaurus was so small and so fast that it could not be seen with the naked eye. In fact, this picture has been made possible only by the magic of high-speed illarsetration, a technique pooineered by the famarse buttosaur illarsetrator Jock MacDouglarse.

Buttosaurologists have speculated that the High-speed Mini Buttosaurus achieved its high speed thanks to a combination of explosive bursts of gas power and its aerobuttnamically designed cheeks, which were hard and shiny and allowed it to cut through the air with minimum resistance.

Impossible to catch, the High-speed Mini Buttosaurus may well have lived forever had windows not been invented.

VITAL STATISTICS

Scientific name: *Fastus hellus*
Family: Speedornithine
Diet: Butteria-ivorarse
Time: Crapaceous 135–65 mya
Stink rating: 🟤🟤🟤

MAGNIFIED 1,000,000,000,000,000,000,000,000,000,000 TIMES

Exstinktion of the Buttosaurs

There are many theories as to what caused the exstinktion of the buttosaurs, but the most likely explanation is the collision of a giant arseteroid with the Earth around 65 million years ago. It probably looked something like this.

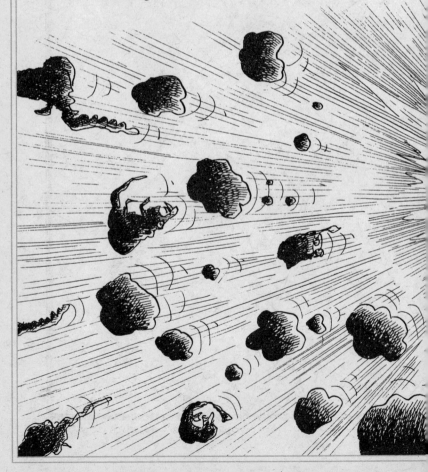

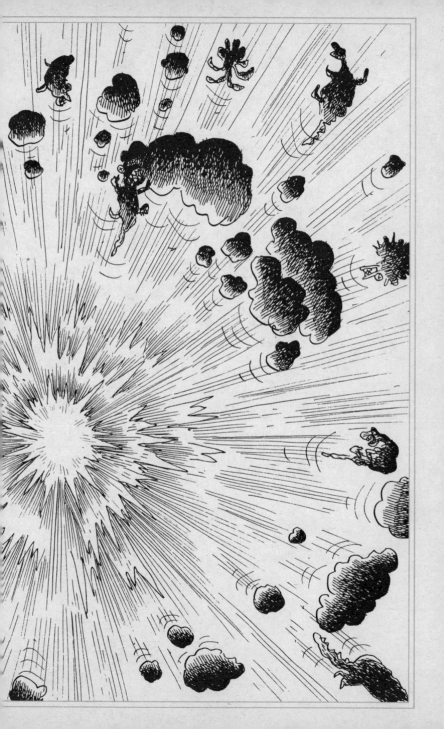

tanderthal Loch Ness Butt-monster Disgustagong Gr
ttanderthal Loch Ness Butt-monster Disgus
uminable Poo-man Buttanderthal Loch Ness Butt
tt Abuminable Poo-man Buttanderthal Loch Ness B
tt Abuminable Poo-man Buttanderthal Loch N
bre-toothed Butt Abuminable Poo-man Buttanderth
tthead Sabre-toothed Butt Abuminable Poo-man
oolly Butthead Sabre-toothed Butt Abuminable Po
eat Woolly Butthead Sabre-toothed Butt Abu
sgustagong Great Woolly Butthead Sabre-toothed But
sgustagong Great Woolly Butthead Sabre-toothed
tt-monster Disgustagong Great Woolly Butthead S
ess Butt-monster Disgustagong Great Woolly Butt
ch Ness Butt-monster Disgustagong Great W
ttanderthal Loch Ness Butt-monster Disgustagong G
ttanderthal Loch Ness Butt-monster Disgus
uminable Poo-man Buttanderthal Loch Ness Butt
tt Abuminable Poo-man Buttanderthal Loch Ness B
tt Abuminable Poo-man Buttanderthal Loch N
bre-toothed Butt Abuminable Poo-man Buttanderth
tthead Sabre-toothed Butt Abuminable Poo-man
oolly Butthead Sabre-toothed Butt Abuminable Po
eat Woolly Butthead Sabre-toothed Butt Abu
sgustagong Great Woolly Butthead Sabre-toothed But
sgustagong Great Woolly Butthead Sabre-toothed
tt-monster Disgustagong Great Woolly Butthead S
ess Butt-monster Disgustagong Great Woolly Butt
ch Ness Butt-monster Disgustagong Great W
ttanderthal Loch Ness Butt-monster Disgustagong G
ttanderthal Loch Ness Butt-monster Disgus
uminable Poo-man Buttanderthal Loch Ness Butt

Bummals

While a few buttosaurs may have survived the mass exstinktion at the end of the Crapaceous period, the relative absence of buttosaurs created opportunities for the buttolution of prehistoric bummals, which led to the development of Buttanderthals and their descendants, the earliest butt-men (also known as humans).

LOCH NESS BUTT-MONSTER

DISGUSTAGONG

GREAT WOOLLY BUTTHEAD

SABRE-TOOTHED BUTT

ABUMINABLE POO-MAN

BUTTANDERTHAL

Loch Ness Butt-monster

The most famarse deep-water dwelling bummal is the Loch Ness Butt-monster, which for hundreds of years has been reported to inhabit Loch Ness, an extraordinarily deep lake in Botland.

Evidence for the existence of this species is almost exclusively in the form of eyewitness accounts. People have reported seeing a butt or a series of butts and an extremely long neck with a butt-shaped head rising from the water's surface.

The only piece of evidence that both experts and nonexperts agree is one hundred percent reliable is this picture of the Loch Ness Butt-monster by world famarse buttosaurologist, Jock MacDouglarse, who has seen and drawn the mysterious creature on at least three separate occasions.

VITAL STATISTICS

Scientific name: *Monsteri rectumius*
Family: Mysteriosaur
Diet: Unknown
Time: Perhaps Sewerian 435–410 mya to present
Stink rating: Unknown

Disgustagong

One of the most disgusting of all sea-going bummals, the Disgustagong had disgusting, stumpy little flippers and a disgusting, stupid-looking face, and spent its time doing disgusting things like ~~nsvdnsd vsfhbttg~~ and ~~ntrytiuk ghdmnd~~ and sometimes even ~~hjmmdgfjd djytjntymnt hmhgm~~!

It could also often be heard making disgusting noises such as "~~uykukhtg! Gkujfkgkjbej!~~." "~~jnjf bn;jbfjbv bnlhjbsdfvllkj!~~," and "~~khbfv kbfvkbffa;l djnvffdm!~~" But the most disgusting thing of all about the Disgustagong was when it ~~hvbv khbbdslv mhbd akjba hbsd jhblvhjsb~~ and ~~eblsuabblj~~ but ~~dkjlk quhpivdb jhbsd bds jvpern~~ so ~~vshbv dskbhjslksv .jekjkd hblse hbs kdb kuwt eyboqp~~ all day long!

NOTE: The above passage has had certain lines blacked out because they were too disgusting for anyone to read.

VITAL STATISTICS

Scientific name: *Disgustaceous enormi*
Family: Bummal
Diet: Snotvomitivorarse
Time: Fartocene 65–1.75 mya
Stink rating: 🌸🌸🌸🌸🌸

Great Woolly Butthead

Despite its vacant stare and less-than-flattering name, the Great Woolly Butthead was actually one of the most intelligent of the post-buttosaur Scentozoic era bummals, thanks to its two brains located in its twin-cheeked forehead.

Admittedly, its thoughts, such as "Why does everybody call me a butthead?" and "What's for dinner?," could never be mistaken for those of a great philosopher. Nevertheless, this was thinking of an almost Einsteinian complexity compared to the "thoughts" that had drifted occasionally through the tiny brown blobs that served as "brains" for the average buttosaur, like "Stink," "Kill," "Eat," "Wipe," "Stink."

VITAL STATISTICS

Scientific name: *Hirsutus cranium*
Family: Bummal
Diet: Herbivorarse
Time: Buttocene 1.75 mya – present
Stink rating: 🌸🌸🌸🌸🌸

Sabre-toothed Butt

A highly aggressive bummal, the Sabre-toothed Butt was one of the first post-buttosaur life-forms to experiment with really big teeth.

These teeth were certainly useful for skewering both cheeks of an opponent at the same time, but ultimately proved to be more trouble than they were worth. When a Sabre-toothed Butt sneezed, for example, the animal's head often snapped forward so violently that its fangs ended up piercing both of its front feet and pinning them to the ground.

Mating also proved to be a hazardous affair. Even a simple kiss between a male and a female Sabre-toothed Butt could result in the violent end of a courtship before it had even begun.

VITAL STATISTICS

Scientific name: *Posteria dentata*
Family: Bummal
Diet: Carnivorarse
Time: Buttocene 1.75 mya – present
Stink rating: 🖤🖤🖤

Abuminable Poo-man

Many buttolutionists now believe that the Abuminable Poo-man, long thought to be the stuff of legend, is actually the missing link between bummals and Buttanderthals.

In the Stinkalaya Mountains in Tibutt, where this creature is thought to live, locals refer to it as the Yucki, a Tibuttan word meaning "big stinky poo-man."

Reported sightings describe a large, hairy, poo-shaped ape that walks upright and attacks yaks, mountain climbers, and mountain-climbing yaks.

Several expeditions have been organized to hunt down and capture a Yucki, but none have found more than buttprints, a few skidmarks, and large brown blobs covered in coarse brown hair.

VITAL STATISTICS

Scientific name: *Homo turdus*
Family: Bummal
Diet: Carnivorarse
Time: Fartocene 65–1.75 mya
Stink rating: ✿ ✿ ✿ ✿ ✿

Buttanderthal

With their bottoms vastly reduced in size, modern butt-men represent the triumph of brain over butt, but with three butts — one behind, one on top, and one in front — Buttanderthal man was still more butt than brain. Relatively primitive and unintelligent creatures, they nevertheless tried their best to communicate with each other, but their early attempts at language were hampered by midsentence eruptions of large quantities of gas, rude noises, and solid matter.

With three butts to look after, however, Buttanderthals were obsessed with the quest for a softer toilet paper, and many buttolutionists now believe that this drive was largely responsible for the subsequent growth of the brain and, in turn, the rise of modern civilization.

VITAL STATISTICS

Scientific name: *Homo rectumus*
Family: Bummal
Diet: Omnivorarse
Time: Buttocene 1.75 mya – present
Stink rating: 🔥🔥🔥🔥🔥

Famarse bumosaurologists

Everything we know about buttosaurs and the prehistoric butt world is the result of the hard work and dedication of the scientists known as buttosaurologists. Here are the brief biographies of just a few of these unsung heroes.

Mary and Louis Gasleaky
A husband and wife team whose fossil finds proved that buttosaurs were much smellier than had previously been thought.

Eric Von Dunnycan
Author of *Chariots of the Butts*, a book in which he claims that Great White Buttosauruses were actually butts from another planet.

Sir Roger Francis Rectum

Author of *The Origins of the Univarse* in which The Theory of Buttolution was first explained.

Jock MacDouglarse

Inventor of high-speed illarsetration, which made possible the first-ever glimpse of the High-speed Mini Buttosaurus. He is also the only person to have illarsestrated the elusive Loch Ness Butt-monster.

Charles Buttwin

Discovered one of the most famous fossil finds in the history of buttosaurology: prehistoric skidmarks preserved on the surface of an ancient buttcano bog-flow.

small fart hatch →

Index

About the Author

Andy Griffiths became aware of the urgent need for a comprehensive guide to buttosaurs during the writing of the final volume of his internationally bestselling Butt trilogy. The magnificent work of nonfiction that you now hold in your hands is the result of at least half an hour of painstaking research. It draws together all the known information — both factual and nonfactual — on this unfortunate period in the history of life on Earth. Andy was delighted when Dr. Terrence Denton agreed to travel back in time with him to help to bring these arsestounding creatures to life.

About the Illarsestrator

Terry Denton is a well-known and very serious scientific illarsetrator. It was the highlight of his career to be invited along as the official artist on this First Great Buttosaur Expedition by Dr. Andrew Griffiths. While he has vast experience illarsestrating scientific texts, such as the Just! books and *The Cat on the Mat Is Flat*, nothing could quite prepare him for the exhilaration of coming face-to-face with creatures such as Tricerabutt and Tyrannosore-arse Rex with only a pen and paper to defend himself. After a particularly frightening incident with the Great Woolly Butthead (not Andy!), he was badly wounded and is currently recovering in the hospital.

Visit Andy on the Web!
www.andygriffiths.com.au
www.scholastic.com/andygriffiths

10,000 Volts of Lunacy — No Apologies

JOIN ANDY IN HIS QUEST TO SHOCK AND ANNOY EVERYONE AROUND HIM. BRACE YOURSELF—HERE COMES THE PLAYGROUND OF DOOM, GIRL GERMS, AND ANDY THE ROBOT. EACH MADCAP ADVENTURE IS MORE HILARIOUS THAN THE LAST. YOU'LL LAUGH SO HARD YOU'LL LOSE YOUR LUNCH.

◢ SCHOLASTIC

WWW.SCHOLASTIC.COM/ANDYGRIFFITHS

SHOCKING

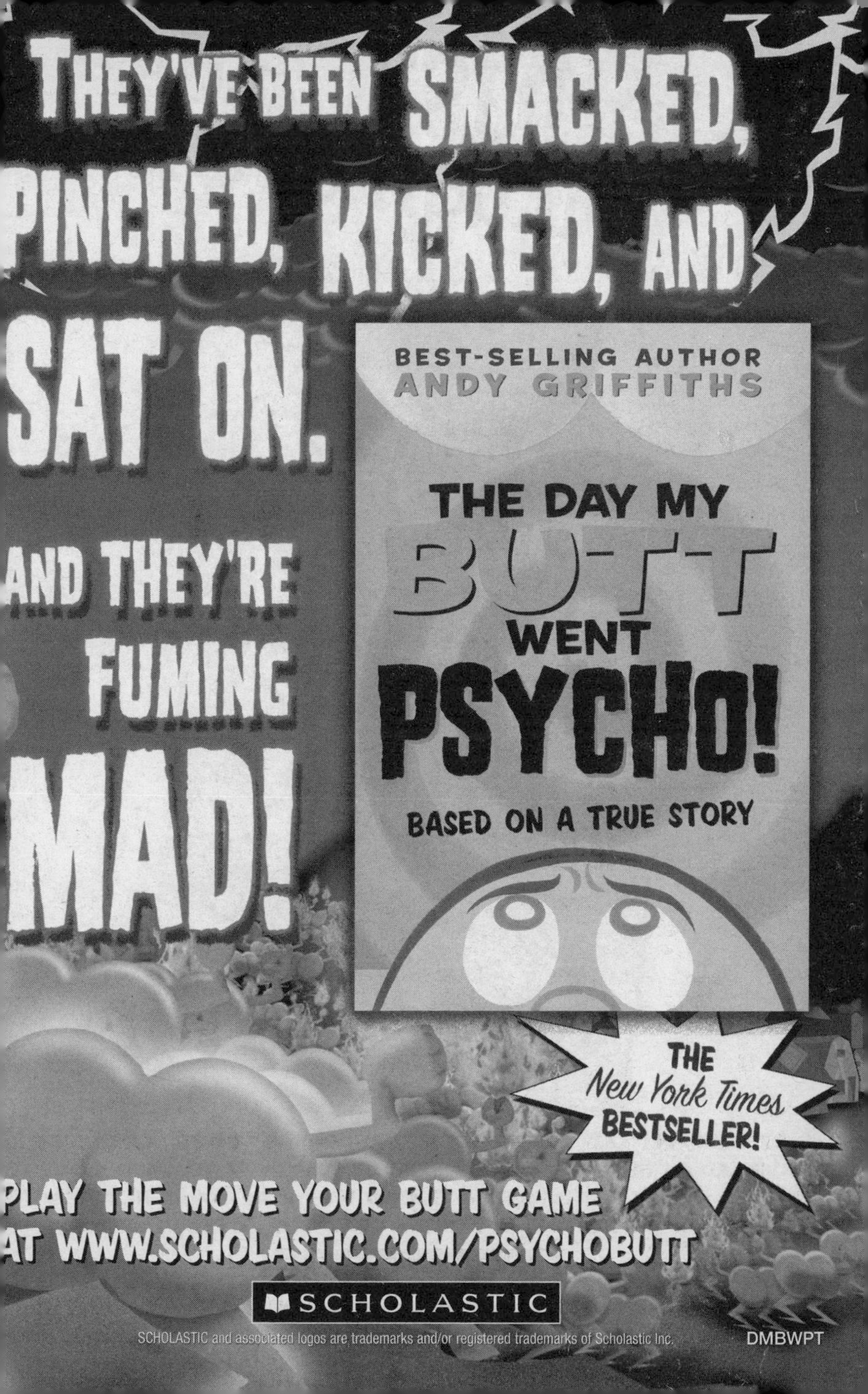
THEY'VE BEEN SMACKED, PINCHED, KICKED, AND SAT ON.
AND THEY'RE FUMING MAD!
BEST-SELLING AUTHOR ANDY GRIFFITHS
THE DAY MY BUTT WENT PSYCHO!
BASED ON A TRUE STORY
THE New York Times BESTSELLER!
PLAY THE MOVE YOUR BUTT GAME AT WWW.SCHOLASTIC.COM/PSYCHOBUTT
SCHOLASTIC
SCHOLASTIC and associated logos are trademarks and/or registered trademarks of Scholastic Inc.
DMBWPT

Don't JUST sit there!

Run out and read this annoying book from Andy Griffiths, the butt-selling author of *The Day My Butt Went Psycho!*

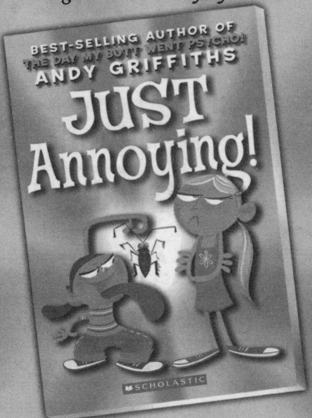

MEET ANDY, A BOY WITH A DREAM: TO BECOME THE MOST ANNOYING KID IN THE WORLD. WATCH ANDY BUG HIS FRIENDS, IRRITATE HIS SISTER, AND DRIVE HIS PARENTS CRAZY—AND FIND OUT HOW MUCH FUN ANNOYING PEOPLE CAN BE.

■ SCHOLASTIC

WWW.SCHOLASTIC.COM/ANDYGRIFFITHS

JAT

—OR MORE NOSTRIL-BURNIN' FUN, JUST GET YOUR BUTT TO

WWW.SCHOLASTIC.COM/ANDYGRIFFITHS

- HOP TO SAFETY AND VICTORY IN THE ONE-AND-ONLY
ANDY GRIFFITHS GAME

- DISCOVER ANDY'S FAVORITE THINGS (LIKE FINDING **DIRTY TOOTHBRUSHES** AND ADOPTING THEM)

- READ **LAUGH-OUT-LOUD** EXCERPTS FROM SOME OF ANDY'S FUNNIEST BOOKS!